What News of the War?

ROBERT BOBER

What News of the War?

TRANSLATED BY
ROBIN BUSS

HAMISH HAMILTON · LONDON

HAMISH HAMILTON LTD

Published by the Penguin Group
Penguin Books Ltd, 27 Wrights Lane, London w 8 5 tz, England
Penguin Putnam Inc., 375 Hudson Street, New York, New York 10014, USA
Penguin Books Australia Ltd, Ringwood, Victoria, Australia
Penguin Books Canada Ltd, 10 Alcorn Avenue, Toronto, Ontario, Canada m 4 v 3 b 2
Penguin Books (NZ) Ltd, 182–190 Wairau Road, Auckland 10, New Zealand

Penguin Books Ltd, Registered Offices: Harmondsworth, Middlesex, England

Quoi de neuf sur la guerre? first published in France by P.O.L. éditeur 1993
This translation first published by Hamish Hamilton Ltd 1998
1 3 5 7 9 10 8 6 4 2

Copyright © Robert Bober, 1993
Translation copyright © Robin Buss, 1998
The moral rights of the author and the translator have been asserted

Set in 12.5/16.5pt Monotype Garamond
Typeset by Rowland Phototypesetting Ltd, Bury St Edmunds, Suffolk
Printed in England by Clays Ltd, St Ives plc

A CIP catalogue record for this book is available from the British Library

ISBN 0–241–13508–7

In memory of my parents

Acknowledgements

This book would probably not have come into being if, between 1947 and 1953, I had not worked in many tailors' shops, first as an apprentice, then as a machinist and finally as a cutter.

So my thanks go in the first place to all those, bosses and workers, with whom I experienced so many busy and slack seasons, in particular to David Grynszpan, Jacques Goroch, Adolphe Knoplioch and Albert Mintz.

My thanks also to my friends Pierre Dumayet, Jean-Claude Grumberg, Paul Otchakovsky-Laurens, Georges Perec, Louba Pludermacher and André Schwarz-Bart, who, in various ways, are present in these stories.

Part One

'Do you know what, Reb Sholem Aleichem,
we'd rather talk about something pleasant:
what news of the war?'

SHOLEM ALEICHEM, *Tevy the Dairyman*

'The war is over, but on no account pass it on.'

Franc-Tireur, 8 May 1945

Abramowicz

My name is Abramowicz, Maurice Abramowicz. Here
in the workshop they call me Abramauschwitz. At first
this was because it made us laugh, but now it's more
out of habit. It was Léon the presser who thought that
up. Not to start with; he wouldn't have dared – because,
when all's said and done, an ex-deportee is first and fore-
most an ex-deportee, even if he's also a good machinist.

As a machinist, I need fear no one, especially where
speed is concerned. When I applied here at the start of
the season, there were two of us after the job. What I
mean is, there were others, who came with the newspaper tucked under their arm, but two of us were already
seated at our machines. The other guy was young and
strong, and from the way he looked at the pattern, I
could see straightaway that he knew what he was doing.
But forty minutes later, when I was finishing off the
second sleeve, he was only just starting to sew on the
collar. When I hung the completed coat on the dummy,

he looked up with a smile and told me that if he'd known I was a 'greener',* he wouldn't even have tried to take me on. The boss paid him for his work and he went off to look for another job. After that, I got to know the workshop.

There are three sewing machines: one for me; another opposite for Charles, a machinist who has known the boss since before the war, but never utters a word; and the third for the boss himself, though he doesn't use it often. He sews the linings and the models. Sometimes he still makes a garment to measure, but his main job is cutting out.

Every week, after he has delivered to Wasserman's, he lays the cloth out on his cutting table and arranges the pattern on top so as to save as much as possible. This is when he sings songs that you don't hear on the radio. He says they are music-hall songs from before the war. Now, his wife, Mme Léa, when she sings, it's in Yiddish. Not that it matters too much, because in the busy season we make so much noise with the machines that you can't hear the singing.

Not that she's always there, Mme Léa, either, with her two children – Raphaël, who is thirteen, and his little sister Betty. A whole family.

*In Yiddish, an immigrant just off the boat. US: 'greenhorn'; French: '*un bleu*'.

We come in to work on Saturdays as well, because everyone needs his job. But on that day, in the afternoon, Mme Léa comes in with tea in tall glasses and some cake which she makes herself. Charles, who never says a word otherwise, says thank you and drinks the piping hot tea in little gulps. Every time, before he goes back to work, he slowly wipes his spectacles.

Mme Léa looks on Charles and me as children. When we've finished, she seems to give a little sigh before taking the glasses back to the kitchen.

The work Charles and I turn out is enough to keep three women occupied finishing off. Here in France I've noticed that finishers are rarely Jewish. I mean, you do sometimes find one who is Jewish, but it's not long before she marries a machinist and the two of them set up on their own.

There is one finisher in the shop, Mme Paulette, who is Jewish, but she's old. She tries to talk like a goy and claims that her accent comes from Alsace, but Léon told me that her Yiddish accent is almost as strong as mine.

The other two finishers are called Jacqueline and Andrée. Andrée is known as Mme Andrée, because she was married, then got divorced. Perhaps that's why she's sad. Not that she's really sad, but she never laughs.

Of course, mostly when we laugh in the shop it's because someone has told a story in Yiddish.

My mother told me that in Szydlowiec, in Poland, her mother always used to say: 'Yiddish is the most beautiful of all languages!'

'How is that?' my mother would ask.

'Rayselé,' her mother replied. 'It's because in Yiddish you can understand every word.'

Still, even when we're speaking French, Madame Andrée doesn't laugh. It's as though she doesn't understand every word in French. You might think that's because of the accent, except that Léon, the presser, was practically born in France and she doesn't laugh with him, either. When he called me Abramauschwitz for the first time, we laughed so much we had to stop working. Mme Andrée went quite white. If I hadn't laughed as well, she would definitely have said something to Léon: one shouldn't joke about such things. For non-Jews to make a joke of it, perhaps, if you must; but not here, not in the shop, not the Jews, who *know.*

Just the other morning already, she came in looking quite pale. She'd heard this entertainer, Jean Rigaux, say a dreadful thing about the camps on the radio: 'That they weren't crematoria, but incubators!' Léon, too, went white. No one in the room said a word; we kept our thoughts to ourselves. I thought, to hell with that Rigaux. M. Albert, the boss, did not sing for the whole day. All we could hear was the noise of the machines and the sound of the steam rising from Léon's cloth when he put his gas iron on it.

I'm fond of Mme Andrée and my heart aches when she turns pale: it's as though you can see right through her, especially with her dark hair. It suits her better when her cheeks are red, which is quite often, since she blushes easily.

In our family we've always liked red cheeks – a sign of good health, my mother used to say. In Poland she would always look enviously at the red cheeks of the Polish girls, with their blond hair, as they walked by on the opposite pavement. She had to relieve her feelings with a curse.

A few days ago Mme Andrée's cheeks were particularly red. She asked me whether, as the slack season was coming, I'd like to make her a winter coat; of course, she would pay me for the work. So that evening, when she had finished sewing in the linings and had taken off her working coat, I took her measurements. She was wearing a white rayon blouse and a very straight black skirt, and stood there in front of me without a word. Bust: 94 cm. I leant down a little. Waist: 67 cm. I bent even further down and put the tape measure around her hips: 100 cm. A perfect 'stockman', size 42.*

I put the note of her measurements in the drawer of

*A type of dummy which was often used by bespoke tailors.

my machine and did a bit more work, thinking about Mme Andrée. Perhaps one day, if I see her laugh when she hears Léon call me Abramauschwitz, I'll ask her if she'd like to set up in business with me.

Raphaël's First Letter

Dear Mama, dear Papa,

I'm writing from the château where we arrived safely. There are a lot of us at summer camp and not enough rooms for everybody in the château so the big ones between thirteen and fifteen that includes me sleep in large tents called 'marabouts'. Betty is sleeping in a round room in the château. We all eat in a big room in the château and the food is better than at the boarding school in Clamart. In that room there is a big organ but no one is allowed to touch it. They told us that the château used to belong to some priests before, but during the war it was requisitioned by the Germans. In the château there is also a hobby room, and that's where I'm writing to you. They make us write a letter once a week but there are some who don't write because they say they have no one to write to. Talking of Clamart, who do you think I've met here at camp? Raphaël the First! You remember, he was with me at boarding school. I told you that he was called Raphaël the First because

9

when I arrived that made two Raphaëls. We bagged beds next
to each other in the tent because we already knew each other.
Now we know our real names. When I told him that I took my
DEPP* under the name 'Blondel' and that I lost a year through
it, we laughed till we cried. Raphaël the First's big sister is a
counsellor at the camp. The supervisors are very nice. They told
us about the Resistance the first evening at the gathering in
the refectory. They taught us the song of the Soviet partisans,
which I know almost all by heart. I'll sing it for you when I get
home.

There's one supervisor whose name is Simon but they call
him Lieutenant because he went with the Army to Berlin.
We're all going to have nicknames according to our character
or some other reason. My supervisor is called Max and he's
going to be a lawyer later on. I forgot to say that we are
split up into groups of about fifteen and every group has a
name. I'm in the Thomas Fogel group. Thomas Fogel was a
member of the Resistance who was shot when he was seventeen. He was a comrade of the supervisors who are with us.
The other groups for the big ones are called Charles Wolmark,
Léon Bursztyn and Marcel Rayman. All of them were shot
by the Germans. Everyone here is on first-name terms. We
even call the director of the camp by her first name. It's Louba,
a Russian name. This afternoon we're going to have a game of

Diplôme de l'enseignement primaire public. primary school
certificate.

ballon prisonnier* and learn some folk dances. If you send me a parcel, put in things that can be divided up because we put all the parcels together and that will make it easier to share them out.

Lots of love and I'm handing over to Betty, who will say a few words,

Raphaël

Lots of love,

Betty

*A game played by schoolchildren involving two teams. The ball is thrown from one to the other and if a player is hit, he is 'taken prisoner' – he has to go to the far end of the ground, behind the opposing team, and can only be released if he manages to catch the ball and hit one of his opponents with it (translator's note).

Raphaël's Second Letter

Dear Mama, dear Papa,

We've been at camp for two weeks now and I'm still enjoying it. I hope you are well too. We do lots of different activities and put on little plays in the evening with a supervisor who does acting and who's nicknamed 'Dram Art'. Here, even peeling vegetables is one of the activities! Every morning it's one group's turn to do the peeling. They told us that this was to help out the kitchen workers who are Spanish Republican refugees who came to France after the Spanish Civil War. So we peel the potatoes and use the time to learn a new song. As well as Raphaël the First, I've made heaps of new friends. One I get on really well with is called Georges. He has a craze, which is making lists, especially lists of films. He asks everybody which films they have seen and writes the titles down on sheets of paper. But he keeps rewriting them because he copies them out in alphabetical order and there are always new ones. So you find lists everywhere – in the rooms, in the tent or in the grounds of the château.

Yesterday something happened while we were doing the wall newspaper. A wall newspaper is a newspaper which you hang up on the wall of the refectory and stick on articles which we've written ourselves, or songs or drawings. They had put a long table out in the grounds with benches and we were each doing a drawing or writing an article when suddenly Max, our supervisor, shouted, 'PAPA!' very loudly and we all looked up. A gentleman with a lady holding his arm was walking very slowly towards us. Then Max ran over to him and kissed him. And all three of them began to weep and hug each other. Then the girl next to me began to weep too and so did some of the others. It was Max's father, who had come back from deportation. That night Georges who sleeps in the same tent as me suddenly woke up shouting. That woke up the rest of us and we realized that the supervisors were not asleep – they were walking around in the tents and in the rooms. This morning we found out that a child had run away during the night and the gendarmes picked him up in his pyjamas at the station. They brought him back and told the supervisors that they were not looking after the children in the camp properly.

The other evening they showed us a Soviet film called The Rainbow. *It was good. It is the story of a village occupied by the Boches, until it was liberated by the Partisans. Georges liked the film, too, except that the French title is* L'Arc-en-ciel, *which means he has to start his list of films all over again from the beginning.*

I must leave you now because I still have to finish the article on the film L'Arc-en-ciel *for the wall newspaper.*

What News of the War?

I forgot to tell you that Betty is very well but I know that she wrote to you when it was her day for letter-writing.

Love and kisses,

Your loving son Raphaël

PS. I got the parcel, but it was not easy to share out the cake because it was a bit squashed in the post.

Raphaël's Third Letter

Manoir de D.

Dear Mama, dear Papa,

Today is letter-writing day again and I have nothing special to tell you about except the fête we are planning at the end of the month. Each group has to build a stand and put on a show for the others and for the people from the village who are invited.

Apart from that, something odd happened last night in our tent. I'm not quite sure how to describe it to you. Georges says that you must always note everything down or tell someone about it so that you will remember it later. He is sitting next to me and is using the letter-writing period to do his list of films over again because he has no one to write to. He suggested that I do a drawing so that I can explain better what happened last night.

Here is a drawing of the tent with the position of each bed.

Last night Marcel got up to go to the toilet and went out of the tent on side A. He didn't put on the light to avoid waking us up but that didn't matter because he knew that his bed was the first on the right as you came in. But I don't know why, for

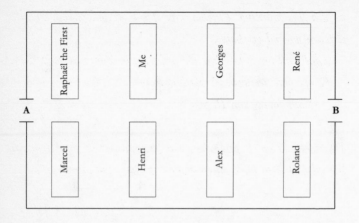

some reason he came back in shortly afterwards from side B and
was very surprised when he got into bed to find someone in it so
he started to shake René who was fast asleep asking what he
was doing there. René didn't know what was going on. Marcel
was convinced that René must have been sleepwalking so he made
him go back to his bed in the opposite corner. There is a lamp
in the grounds which stays on all night and it was shining on
Marcel's bed which really was empty. At that moment we woke
up in time to see René apologizing and getting into Marcel's bed.
Raphaël the First put on the light to find out what was going on
and saw Marcel in René's bed and René in Marcel's. And when
the light went on, Marcel realized his mistake. We all burst out
laughing except René who was angry and claimed the whole tent
had played a trick on him. Max came in but we were laughing
so much that we couldn't explain what had happened. So to calm
us down he said we could peel the potatoes again which is what

we did this morning. I'm not sure if you've understood, but I'll explain when I get home.

That's all for today, but I'll write again before we leave here. I hope you are well. A big hug from

Your loving son Raphaël

P.S. Betty is not happy when you write to her in your letters to me. She likes to have an envelope with her own name on it.

Raphaël's Fourth Letter

Manoir de D.

Dear Mama, dear Papa,

This is the last letter I'll be writing because we go back to Paris in three days.

Yesterday we had the big fête for the end of the summer camp and it was terrific. Lots of people came from the village and also some from Paris. The grounds had been decorated with streamers and garlands and there were stalls like the ones in a fairground. The stalls for the little ones were games and Betty was looking after a lottery with a spinning wheel made out of a bicycle wheel.

To begin with the choir of the older ones sang on the front steps of the château. We sang three songs in harmony, in French: the song of the Marais, the song of the Soviet Partisans and the song of the French Partisans. After that we sang the song of the Jewish Partisans in Yiddish. When we sang that everyone stood up though the people from the village didn't at first because they didn't know what it was. After that each group staged a show on its stand.

There were choral recitations. A choral recitation is a poem spoken by a group, but not all at once. Each person says one or two lines, or else the group is split in two and you take turns. My group did a choral recitation of a poem by René Guy Cadou, Les Fusillés de Châteaubriant, *about those who were executed at Châteaubriant. At the end of the poem I said two lines by myself:*

> *How simple everything is*
> *And death most of all is a simple thing*

then we all said together:

> *Since every freedom outlives itself.*

The two groups of older ones acted plays in Yiddish. There was one by Sholem Aleichem and another, La Réforme, *which was written and performed in 1942 at the concentration camp at Pithiviers.*

But the best of all was the show of tableaux vivants put on by 'Dram Art'. This was a series of mimes illustrating events in the Resistance from Colonel Fabien's attack at the Barbès metro station to the barricades during the Liberation of Paris. At the back there was a group reciting a poem by Aragon, La Rose et le Réséda *and Paul Eluard's* Courage. *And 'Dram Art' played the mouth-organ while they were performing the scenes at the front. The people who had come from Paris started to cry. After that there was a high tea and Louba, the director, introduced someone who made a speech and told us that a lot of children* would stay at the Manoir after the holidays. They are all the children whose parents are still not back from the camps. A bus will come every day to take them to school, since it is too far for them to walk. The little ones will go to the village school. Georges, who is staying as well, will sleep in the château. I told him it was great, the ones who stayed would feel as though they were still on holiday. But he wasn't so sure. Perhaps his parents will come back soon. I promised to write to him and to send him cinema programmes for his list. If they still have a letter-writing day, now he'll have someone to write to.

Well, tomorrow we have to clear up the grounds so that it is tidy when we leave and someone will weigh us to see if we've fattened up over the summer.

If you come to meet us at the station, we will be arriving at 4.30 in the afternoon at the Gare Saint-Lazare.

With much love and kisses,

Raphaël

'Doing and Undoing
is Also Work'

Léon has come back to work. He left for a season to set up on his own. M. Albert wished him good luck, adding, 'If it doesn't work out, you can always come back.' And he did.

When he left, he said, just as he did every evening: '*Ich four avek Sénégalais.*'* To set himself up, he borrowed a sewing machine, bought a dummy and settled down in his dining room. So? The table was an old pressing table anyway. He did everything himself, except his wife sewed in the linings. He also did the deliveries, once

---

*A double pun. *Ich four avek* means 'I'm off'. This can be colloquially translated in French by *je me tire ailleurs*, which suggests *tirailleur* ('infantryman'). *Les tirailleurs sénégalais* were French colonial troops. There is a further pun at the end of the chapter, where Léon says that he is leaving, because it is *plus bath ailleurs* ('more fun elsewhere', perhaps) – but also a pun on *batailleur* ('rowdy') (translator's note).

or twice a week, to Lederman's in the Faubourg-Poissonnière.

The season went by here without Léon. In his place, M. Albert hired a young presser called Joseph. From his manner of speaking you could see that he was well-educated, but he didn't iron as well as Léon. In the evening when he had left, M. Albert sometimes had to pick up the iron himself, to puff out the top of a sleeve or take the shine off a lapel. But he said nothing to Joseph because he liked him.

When Léon came back with his dummy under his arm, we had one presser too many in the shop. That evening M. Albert had a long talk with Joseph in the kitchen and a week later Léon was back at his place behind the pressing table.

The first morning, I greeted him with: 'Are you back then, Senegalese?'

'Abramauschwitz,' he said, looking me straight in the eye. 'Abramauschwitz!' From his look, I realized that he was trying to tell me that he was the one who did the funnies in the shop. 'A Senegalese doesn't come back, a Senegalese *four avek.*'

After that no one dared ask him what went wrong with Lederman. When Jacqueline, the little finisher who likes a joke, ventured, 'So, Monsieur Léon, was it because you missed me that you came back?', Léon just answered with a nod and a smile.

We had to wait a week before Léon told us what had happened.

All had gone well during the season. We already knew that he had done everything himself, except that his wife did the finishing off for him; since they have a small boy who is not yet at school, because he was born in 1942, they had plenty to fill the day. And the evening, and even some Saturdays. 'More than once,' Léon told us, 'I got up in the morning with piping round my eyes.'

Then the slack season came to Lederman's, as it does to everyone. And Lederman, who up to then had been sending coats to the shops almost without looking at them, started to hunt for trifling faults in the clothes. 'These are new season models,' he would say, 'and if the models don't hang right, then the whole season's a write-off.' Also, to hold on to the tailors who worked for him, he divided the new designs up among them all.

Four times already Léon had gone home with just one jacket to make. And, twice out of those four times, Lederman had sent the garment back to be put right. The first time it was a lining that was too tight, the second a sleeve wrongly set. Not that it was true, Léon assured us. On M. Albert's advice, he had agreed not to argue about it, and had simply gone home and run an iron over the jacket. 'You see,' Lederman had said triumphantly each time, 'now it falls right.'

Then, just over a week ago, Léon was delivering a checked jacket (the kind that drives us crazy here because of matching the checks), and on the stairs he met an old tailor sadly coming down with a black percaline outfit over his shoulder.

Léon looked enquiringly at the old man.

'This is the second time he's sent it back,' the man told him.

'But everyone says you have golden hands,' Léon exclaimed.

'I may have the golden hands, but he's the one who gives out the work.'

By the time Léon reached Lederman's door, he felt as angry as the old man: it was disgusting, daring to send back a garment twice in a row to old Vilner on the grounds that you are higher up the ladder than he is.

He put the outfit down on the front table and calmly, even though his hands were trembling a little, he undid the safety pins. Without a word, Lederman took the jacket, hung it on the stockman and immediately, while the sleeves were still moving, snapped, 'It doesn't fall right!'

At this point in the story, Léon became as nervous as he had been at Lederman's and we almost stopped work to hear what he was going to say next – except for Mme Paulette, who doesn't like Léon because he never misses the opportunity to tell her she's in the wrong, if she is.

'Doesn't fall right? Doesn't fall right?' Léon yelled. 'We'll see if it doesn't fall right!' And he pulled the jacket off the dummy.

While he was telling us this, here in M. Albert's workshop, Léon took down the jacket he had just finished ironing and strode across the floor, passing in front of Mme Paulette, who suddenly raised her head with a look of fright: but he went straight to the window, opened it wide and, hup, made as if to throw the jacket out.

'And I threw the jacket into the Faubourg-Poissonnière,' Léon went on, suddenly quite calm, 'from the third floor of Lederman's, the dressmaker.'

At this, because Léon is a good storyteller, I saw that M. Albert was uneasy, because he thought that Léon was really going to drop the jacket he was holding, even though the workshop here is only on the first floor and overlooks a courtyard.

'So, what then?' M. Albert asked.

Léon replaced the jacket on the dummy and gave a huge smile, as though he could see it all in his mind, and he told us that, while the piece was falling – and taking its time, because the sleeves filled with air – Lederman seemed to be running around in circles, shouting. And all one could gather from what he was shouting, was, 'My model! My model!' To which Léon replied, 'It falls well, it falls just right.'

First Lederman leapt to the window, as if to verify what Léon was saying, then he dashed down the stairs, taking them four steps at a time, still yelling, 'My model! My model!' Léon looked out of the window and saw old Vilner, who had looked up because of the noise. And old Vilner was amazed because, though in a long life he had seen many things falling out of windows, this was the first jacket with a Prince-of-Wales check.

Of course, Léon shouldn't have done it. He could have lost his temper and told Lederman a few home truths. But no doubt Léon guessed that Lederman already knew these home truths, whereas he had never had the chance to see how a garment falls really well.

'Listen, Monsieur Lederman,' Léon might have said, 'I have been in the trade long enough to know about the slack season. It existed before you came into the world and will still be with us when my son is old enough to go out to work – except that he will never be a tailor. It's so that he will not be a tailor that I have worked my fingers to the bone day and night. So if there's no work, tell me honestly that there's no work, even if it breaks your heart to turn me away empty-handed and to let me go without work for a day or two. It's not the war any longer, Monsieur Lederman' (and here Léon might have raised his voice), 'and I've earned the right to go for a walk in the park with my wife and son. So don't ever again make me redo the work just so that you can keep me for the busy season.'

This would have given Lederman the opportunity to talk about the war, and perhaps they would have changed the subject. But Léon preferred to sum it all up with, 'So it doesn't fall right? Hup! Out of the window. Now it falls well.'

I must say, I'd like to have seen it. To have seen Lederman's face as he yelled, 'My model!' To have seen him running down the stairs and to have seen the jacket falling from the window, and also M. Vilner's face as he watched a bird in a Prince-of-Wales check flying through the air above the Faubourg-Poissonnière.

There you have it. That was the end of the story of Léon and Lederman except that, some time later, M. Albert came into the workshop with a delivery and a question for Léon. At Wasserman's he had bumped into some outworkers who also worked for Lederman and who knew enough about the 'jacket-falling-right' to tell the story themselves. But no one could make out something that Lederman himself didn't understand: what Léon had said just before he slammed the door.

'So, Léon,' M. Albert asked, 'what was it you said to Lederman?'

'I told him,' Léon said, quietly putting down his gas iron to give himself time, 'I told him: "*Ich four avek* because things are hotting up out there!"'*

*See footnote on p. 21.

'Hello-hello'

'If I survived during the Occupation, it was thanks to a tailor in the Rue de Sèvres.' M. Albert was talking to Abramowicz, because Charles and I already knew the story he was telling.

'My wife was with the little one, hiding in the country, but they wouldn't take Raphaël and me. We sent Raphaël to boarding school under a false name; as for me, this tailor in the Rue de Sèvres put me in an attic room in the apartment building where he still has his shop. There was no good cloth to be had at the time, even for the well-off ones around there, so they came to have their clothes remade. A coat could be turned into a jacket, a man's suit became a child's suit or a woman's jacket, because cloth made before the war was not like it is now – it would last for years. I had learned how to measure up first in Poland, then in Berlin in a large firm, and when I had finished working on a garment, no one could tell if it was brand new or remade. M. Dumaillet, the tailor, would do the fittings, and then late in the evening he would bring up the work for me with some food. We agreed on a signal, so that I would not open up for just anybody. He would knock three times, wait for a minute, then say a password that changed every evening: "Braid", "Piping", "Culottes", "Ribbon", "Rayon", "Buttonhole", "Epaulette", "Shoulderpad" – we got through the whole vocabulary of the trade. As soon as I heard steps coming up the stairs, I would take my cutting-out scissors and hide behind the door, ready to defend my life.'

When he reached this part about defending his life, M. Albert was like someone on the stage. He got down behind the door and, with a dreadful look, was holding his big pair of cutting scissors above his head, ready to go on with the story. Well, this was the very moment that Mme Sarah chose to come into the room. Rudely interrupted in his narrative, M. Albert stayed there, saying nothing, but with the scissors poised above his head, holding them in both hands.

Mme Sarah's face took on a look that it must often have worn and she rushed out, shouting, '*Gevalt!*'* before anyone had a chance to tell her that she had not stumbled into the midst of a pogrom.

Mme Sarah's *gevalt!* brought Mme Léa out of her

---

*'Help!'

kitchen so fast that she caught a glimpse of her husband, still brandishing the scissors above his head.

'It was "Hello-hello",' M. Albert said, as if to justify his action.

'What did she do?'

'She took fright and ran.'

'Did you threaten her? Why did you threaten her?'

'I didn't. I was telling Maurice a story. She didn't get as far as saying, "Hello-hello"; she gave a cry and took to her heels. That's all.'

'You and your stories! And now I suppose you have to frighten Mme Sarah before you can tell them?'

In spite of the steam, from across the room I could tell from the colour of M. Albert's face that he was annoyed, because if there's one thing he can't stand, it's Mme Léa telling him off in front of us. But what M. Albert found really unbearable this time was that Mme Léa was telling him off when he was the star of the show, and we wondered if he would ever have a chance to finish his story. He had no alternative but to go back to his cutting table and give vent to his irritation before he went on tracing out a stack of linings.

'She'll be back, she'll be back! Do you want to go running after her? Go on, then! She needs us. Do you think she can find many people as stupid as we are to buy her rotten soap?'

Mme Léa was prevented from answering by the arrival

of Jacqueline and Mme Andrée. We just caught the look that she gave her husband before she left the room, while I motioned to the finishers to stop asking me questions with their eyes.

Mme Sarah, who must be around five feet tall, is undoubtedly the fastest and most agile woman of her age that I have ever encountered – though I don't know anyone who could actually put an age to her. Every month she comes to the shop to sell us soap and candles. When we see her at the door, carrying the little suitcase with the frayed corners that she uses to transport her goods in, and when she looks at us with her grey eyes, and also her slightly grey hair, carelessly stuffed under the shawl that she wears winter and summer, it is enough to make us wonder if the war is really over.

She is known everywhere around the Rue de Turenne, that is the Rue de Turenne itself and the roads leading into it, where you can hear the hum of sewing machines all day long.

Before the war her husband was the *shammes** of a little synagogue in the Rue des Rosiers. In July 1942 he was still carrying out his duties and insisted on opening the synagogue every morning.

Mme Sarah begged him to take off his shawl and have his beard shaved: 'A Jew without a beard is better

*Caretaker, assistant to a rabbi.

than a beard without a Jew!' But he trusted in divine justice, right up to the morning when another form of justice despatched him to Drancy* with the key to the synagogue in his pocket.

To begin with, apart from her cup of tea in the kitchen with Mme Léa, Mme Sarah came to the workshop solely in order to sell her candles and soap. But for some time she had exercised the traditional profession of marriage broker. Her visits to the different cutting rooms in the district brought her into contact with a lot of people who had been left free to marry by the epidemic that broke out around the time when Jews were forced to sew a yellow star above their left breast. But in the main, these people were still hoping and waiting, and Mme Sarah, who had made up her mind to dedicate herself to their happiness, waited too.

Mme Sarah kept her list of eligible people in the inner pocket of her suitcase. There were two envelopes, each with an elastic band around it. The first contained some filing cards, with a name and a few details, such as age and profession. These were the names of those who thought that life would be easier if they were married, which is why there was also a little photograph stuck

*Site of a notorious transfer camp outside Paris where Jews were rounded up and held before being sent on to the death camps (translator's note).

on some of the cards. In the other envelope there was a long list of names among which I was surprised, one day when I asked to have a look at it, to see the names of Charles and Maurice.

I realized that this was a list of people for whose future Mme Sarah was hoping to make plans. I tried to make a casual remark: 'Your list of those eligible for marriage smells of soap, Madame Sarah.' This was true, as it happened.

'Did you prefer it when it was the soap that smelled of those eligible for marriage, Monsieur Léon?'

For once I was left speechless, because anyone here will tell you that nobody, not even I, has ever dared to make a joke about soap. I handed back her list of prospective names and took up my iron.

Amongst ourselves, we called Mme Sarah 'Hello-hello', because '*bonjour*' was pretty well the only word she knew in French. She would often say it twice in succession as she came through the workshop door (hence her nickname), then the rest of the conversation would be in Yiddish. However, she did understand French, because Mme Andrée, who was a kindly soul but didn't speak Yiddish, bought soap from her, even though it was no cheaper or better than any other.

One day, after drinking her tea with Mme Léa, Mme Sarah felt enough at her ease to talk to Abramowicz about some young women of excellent family who, she claimed, 'had never yet allowed themselves to be approached'. When Mme Sarah said that a girl had 'allowed herself to be approached', this meant that the girl had been loved from head to foot already.

But Mme Sarah, who no longer even had the good taste to put sugar in her tea, was not endowed with the kind of clients she was describing to Maurice. In short, that was not her speciality. One doesn't take up haute couture once one is doing off-the-peg; and, as I mentioned earlier, with her shawl and her grey eyes, Madame Sarah spoke of the war without so much as having to open her mouth.

Another time Madame Sarah silently put down a few cards on Charles's machine and waited.

'Take your cards away, Madame Sarah,' Charles said, without looking either at the cards or at her.

'At least look at the photos,' Mme Sarah said, not moving. 'At least do that for me.'

Charles stopped working the machine. 'So, now it's for you that I have to get married? That's something new, Madame Sarah,' he went on, very calmly. 'If you want to marry people, that's one thing, and if you need to make a living, that's another, but don't confuse the two. One, you perform a *mitzvah** and you turn a page.

*Divine commandment; by extension a good deed.

35

Two, it brings you some money, and you turn another page. You cannot exchange happiness for money, Madame Sarah. Money is separate and extra.'

It occurred to me that Charles could have been a rabbi. But Mme Sarah can't have been listening carefully, or else she was certain that among her cards was the pearl that Charles could not pass by, because she didn't stop.

Whereupon Charles raised his voice. He didn't talk any louder than M. Albert or I do when we speak loudly, but, coming from Charles, it sounded like a yell.

'Madame Sarah, don't ever speak to me about marriage again. Do you hear, Madame Sarah?' And he repeated it, even louder: 'Never speak about marriage again!'

At this Mme Sarah must have realized what Charles had been telling her all along, because she picked up her cards and, without saying a word, she carefully put them back in the envelope with the elastic band around it, and slowly returned it to its usual place in the little brown suitcase. We heard her sniff, and while she was looking for a handkerchief in her coat pocket, Charles was wiping his spectacles with a bit of lining – and you didn't need to look closely to see that it was the inside more than the outside he was wiping.

That day Mme Sarah left the room without making

anyone happy, just as she did on that other occasion
when her 'Hello-hello' stuck in her throat and became
'Gevalt!'

Commemoration

If there's one thing a mother can say, it's when she's proud of her child. You should see how well Raphaël can draw. I could almost say that it's worth coming a long way to see his drawings, especially the ones he does in colour. That's why I was so angry with him for letting his fingers get pinched in the door of the cupboard in his bedroom, and why I slapped him and Betty, who was pushing the door as hard as she could, because (so he told me) he wanted to 'test his resistance to pain'. I ask you, is there a mother who could bear to see her child suffer, even if he wasn't an artist, like my Raphaël? Of course not.

It all happened last week. On Sunday they held a huge demonstration at the Mutualité* on the anniversary of the liberation of Auschwitz. A delegation of children

*The Palais de la Mutualité, on the Left Bank, was a hall used for meetings and rallies (translator's note).

of deportees came from the château where Raphaël and Betty went on holiday, and Raphaël asked if his friend Georges, who was one of those in the delegation, could stay the night with us.

It was all arranged. Georges would sleep in Betty's bed and Betty would come into our bed, with Albert and me.

On Saturday Raphaël went to fetch Georges from the Gare Saint-Lazare and they got home at tea time. I tried to make everything very ordinary because of what Raphaël told me in the letters that he sent us in the summer, but when I saw that Georges didn't know whether he should shake my hand or kiss me, I felt a great weight on my heart and asked myself what kind of a world it is where a child hasn't even got a mother to kiss.

Betty was drinking her cocoa and I'd set out two bowls for Raphaël and Georges. While they were washing their hands, I put the milk on, then I made some bread and jam.

Raphaël sat down and, as Georges was still standing, he told him to do the same.

'I don't want any jam,' Georges said quietly, still standing.

'Don't you want to sit down?' I asked, pouring out the cocoa.

Georges gave Raphaël a look of desperation.

'He doesn't want any jam,' Betty said with her mouth full.

I tried to persuade him. 'You know, it's very good. It's strawberry jam. We brought it from the country.'

'No, no, I don't want any,' Georges answered, speaking very fast and grasping the back of the chair with both hands.

We stared at him, all three of us. He looked as though he was about to be sick.

What could I do? I took the jar of jam off the table and left the children by themselves in the kitchen.

That night when Albert came to bed, he put on his pyjama trousers, because Betty was sleeping between the two of us in our double bed. I held Betty in my arms, and she hugged her teddy bear, who had been in our bed since the morning, so that he could get used to it.

Of course I couldn't sleep, and I found myself crying softly because Betty was lying against my breast just as she used to in the years when the family was apart. I was fine, but I was thinking of the two boys in their room.

I had to wait a week before Raphaël told me the story.

First, he told me that in the darkness Georges asked him whether he was asleep – just as Betty does every evening, because she is afraid of being the last to fall asleep.

Then Raphaël went on:

'Of course I wasn't asleep – we had too much to say to one another for me to go to sleep, even though we had said nothing so far and the light had been out for a good ten minutes. Before that we read for a while, and it was rather like being back at the holiday camp, except that there Georges slept on my right. He was very pleased with the pre-war cinema magazines that Uncle Isidore gave me for him.

'When I said I was awake, Georges waited for a little longer in the darkness. Then he started to speak. It was the first time I had heard him talk at such length. It was a story about the war; something that happened to him:

'"I used to live with my parents in the Rue Julien-Lacroix, in Belleville. I remember there were two rooms . . . In one, the larger one, we ate and washed, my mother did the cooking and I did my homework. We slept in the other room. There was a big bed for my parents and a cot, which was starting to get too small for me. Perhaps that's why I would sometimes get into their bed in the mornings . . . Most of the time, though, they were already up . . . My mother took in sewing – there was a sewing machine in the large room – but my father didn't work from home . . . One day my father came back with a huge jar of jam. He was very pleased

41

and wanted us to eat it that same evening, but my mother said no. She said it was a luxury and we'd do better to wait for the worse times to come, so we could enjoy it all the more . . . My father said that the times were bad enough already, but my mother called my father a glutton and put the jam away in a large wall cupboard, which is where we generally stored our food.

' "One morning, very early – this was in 1942 – there was a loud knock on the door. It was the police. I was still in bed . . . My father instantly swept me up in his arms and put me in the cupboard and said: Don't move, don't say a word! I had never seen him like that before. He was quite pale. He shut the door of the cupboard, but left it slightly ajar so that I could breathe. I saw everything through the gap . . . I saw three policemen come in; they were talking about taking my parents away . . . My father got a suitcase from underneath the wardrobe and packed some things in it. I could not see my mother clearly: it was as though my father was deliberately putting himself between me and her so that she couldn't see me. I didn't dare move, because I was afraid and also because of my father's stern voice. I was nine and not big, so it was easy for me not to move, but I don't know what I was most afraid of: staying hidden or being found . . . When they went out, one of the policemen was carrying the case. My mother was weeping and my father was holding her arm . . .

'"When they had gone, I think I must have stayed in the cupboard for a long time before I dared to come out. I was weeping silently. Then I saw beside me the jar of jam that my father had brought back one evening, so I opened it and, using my finger, without coming out of the cupboard, I ate all the jam in the jar ... A long time after that, though I can't tell you how long, I came out of the cupboard and got dressed. There was no point in staying at home, so I went into the street and almost immediately I threw the whole lot up again. It was then that a woman who knew me took me to her house and looked after me ..."'

This is where Raphaël ended the story, because this must have been where Georges stopped speaking. All I know is that the next morning Raphaël showed Georges the Lycée Charlemagne where he goes to school, and in the afternoon, as planned, they went to the Mutualité for the commemoration. After that, they were going straight on to the station, so Georges took his things and Isy's magazines with him. Betty kissed him goodbye, so I could as well, and I said that he could come back whenever he liked, there would always be a bed for him. But who knows what's the right thing to say?

It was after he had taken Georges to the station that Raphaël asked Betty to pinch his fingers hard in the bedroom cupboard. Only now do I realize that he

43

needed to suffer like Georges, who had become his best friend. And he needed to share some of the pain.

What mother could be more proud of her son? And there was me choosing that moment to slap him – and Betty, too, for good measure.

So I took Raphaël in my arms and, even though he is thirteen, I sat him on my lap, and because one can never find the words when one's heart is full, I made him rest his head against me and I kissed him in silence. Only then did he start to weep. And because his eyes had been full of tears for a whole week, we stayed like that for a long time, the two of us, as though he was still just a little boy.

Letter from Georges

Manoir de D.

Dear Raphaël,

For several days now I have been meaning to write and thank you for the Complete Films *magazines that you gave me when I came to Paris. I read one almost every evening and sometimes I re-read bits. There is one I really like, and remember seeing with my parents at the Cocorico cinema in the Boulevard de Belleville: it's* L'Enfer des anges, *with Louise Carletti. At the beginning of the film, she says: 'My name is Lucette and I'm fourteen years old,' and at the end she dies by jumping into the Seine. She was wearing a cloak with a hood and she had escaped from a remand home. In* Complete Films *they call it Fresnes, but I think Fresnes is a prison, not a remand home.*

I also remember that evening when I was in bed I cried silently, because, as I told you, I used to sleep in the same room as my parents.

I'd like to tell you something else which I haven't said to anyone else. You'll see, it's quite silly, but I'm better now. I cried that evening not because the film was sad (I knew it was only a film), but because I was in love with Louise Carletti and, as I was nine years old, I didn't know what to do – I realized that I would never be able to marry her on account of the age difference.

You can imagine how pleased I was when you gave me the magazine, because afterwards I thought about her a lot, until yesterday evening when Mireille, our new group leader, came to say goodnight to us in our dormitory. She glanced through the magazines and told me that a lot of actors collaborated with the Germans during the war. I asked her to give me some examples, as I didn't dare mention Louise Carletti directly, and she said: Tino Rossi, Sacha Guitry, Maurice Chevalier, Le Vigan, Pierre Fresnay . . . Since there was a photo of Louise Carletti in front of me (the one on the back of Clodoche *with Jules Berry and Pierre Larquey), I had an excuse for asking the question, and she answered yes, she thought so, her too.*

Before I went to sleep, I looked at the photo of Louise Carletti for a long time, and I realized it was over: I'm not in love any more. Otherwise, I don't think I would have dared to write to you.

Oddly, it makes me a little sad, not because of what Mireille told me, but it's as if I'm the one who is no longer loved. I won't pin up Louise Carletti's photo as I was going to.

Talking about photos, I saw that you had some copies of Droit et Liberté *at home. In next week's issue there is meant to be a photo of the Manoir, because last Sunday Marc Chagall (a famous painter) came to see us. They took several pictures with* all of us around him. He gave a painting which is to be the first prize, I think, in a raffle which they are holding for children's homes.

I mentioned Mireille, who is our new group leader. I like her a lot. In the evening she stays for a long time in the dormitories and chats with us. I hope she will stay here, because the problem with group leaders is that they change rather too often.

I hope we'll soon be able to see each other again, perhaps when they have the raffle.

Meanwhile, lots of love,

Georges

Life Tells Me a Story

Now why did Mme Andrée agree to go out with me that evening? Because she lives alone? But doesn't she live alone the rest of the time? Yes, but the rest of the time I haven't invited her. And why did I invite her? Is it proper for a married man, and a father, to invite a woman who is not his wife out to dinner with him? No, it isn't.

Two days ago Léa left with the children to visit her cousin in Brussels. Thanks be to God, he survived the war and so did we, and Brussels is not so far that two cousins can't meet and embrace after being so long apart.

Yesterday evening Mme Andrée stayed rather late at the shop and of course we got talking, until, one thing leading to another, I heard myself inviting her to dinner at a restaurant. She said yes, which was the biggest surprise I'd had that day. Admittedly, it's more agreeable when you don't have to eat alone.

Mme Andrée got changed before we went out. She put on the coat that Abramowicz made to measure for her. It wasn't until she was sitting opposite me on the chair the waiter brought for her, and she smiled, that I realized she looked like Maria Montez. That was also the moment when it occurred to me that I should have to find something to talk about, because of course I don't look like Jean-Pierre Aumont.

Now then, what is there to talk about? What do people usually talk about? Work? Family? We can't talk about work on our evening out, can we? No one cares about work when they're not at work. The family, then? That would be very smart: talking about Léa and the kids with Mme Andée on the one evening when I take her out to dinner. Well, what do I talk about with Léa? That's just it: about work and the family. In the mean time Mme Andrée has finished reading the menu, we are about to order and I urgently need to find something to say before she dismisses me as an idiot. What can she think of me? In the shop I'm M. Albert, who gives her work while she turns the garments inside out and sews in the linings; I pay her regularly every week and that's how it goes, year by year. That's how things are in the workshop, but what about here, in the restaurant? If only they had brought the food, at least we could eat.

Anna Karenina! Yes, I'm sure enough goes on in *Anna Karenina* to keep a conversation going for a whole evening. The trouble is, here I am in the restaurant with Mme Andrée sitting opposite me – so am I going to say: 'Excuse me, Madame Andrée, would you mind if we came back in a week's time – just long enough to read *Anna Karenina*, and I guarantee we'll have a most interesting talk?' Now, that really would make me look like a schmuck.

Well, then, since we're not here just to say hello, goodnight, and see you tomorrow, I look across at her just at the moment when she lowers her own eyes – which is quite natural, since in the shop it's usually Jacqueline who has her nose in the air and a story to tell.

While she's staring at her plate, I can observe her at my leisure.

Perhaps she feels fine like this: who said we were under any obligation to talk! We're easy, all's well, there are white cloths on the tables and two glasses at each place setting.

Then I suddenly find I have a new reason to keep quiet, and it proves that at the moment I'm entitled to a surprise every day. You think you know about life, then one day, from across a table in a restaurant, you learn more than you could by reading the papers.

Mme Andrée starts to tell me about her sister in Angers during the war. Her sister was seventeen at the time. 'And of course,' Mme Andrée says, 'at seventeen you're still a child, you don't always know what you're doing.' And she told me what her sister did, which was to get pregnant. Pregnant by a German soldier. 'You see, Monsieur Albert, what did she understand about the war? She didn't know the first thing about war. She didn't even notice the colour of the uniform. She was in love for the first time. You know how it is, they met out dancing and then saw each other again. They found out about love together. He was only a kid himself . . . eighteen. They didn't consider the consequences. Of course, when the Americans came, he took to his heels with the rest of them. He was scared . . . It's natural at his age. And my sister was left all alone holding a baby only a few months old.'

What's this Madame Andrée is telling me? What's got into her? Weren't we happy enough, just now, saying nothing? What is this war she's telling me about? Haven't I had enough of my own war, without having to listen to someone else's.

But it's not yet the end of the story. In fact, it's just the beginning. We've only got to the Liberation.

'At the Liberation, my sister's head was shaved and they made her walk through the streets naked, with others who were also shaved and stripped bare. With my mother running after her holding a coat, trying to cover her daughter, in spite of the people shouting, while my father was at home, struck dumb with shame, and I was clasping the baby, because I was afraid for him. The German soldier's baby. My husband said he wanted none of that in his family and he walked out on me. We got a divorce and I came to Paris. Back home, the baby is starting to walk now. She's a little girl. My father still doesn't speak. He nearly died of shame.'

Yes, but he didn't die, did he? Some people really died, and not those who 'nearly' did! Would Mme Andrée like to hear the names of a few? We can start right there in the workshop: Charles's wife and daughters, for example, and all of Maurice's family – yes, Maurice, who made her coat! Let her ask 'Hello-hello' to open her suitcase, and she will find a whole list of dead people inside it! But, of course, I don't say all this to Mme Andrée, because I can see the tears running down her cheeks and she doesn't even bother to wipe them away, it's so hard for her to speak. At that moment I think how glad I am we didn't choose a Jewish restaurant, because I would certainly have met someone I knew, and that person, believe me, would have had something to tell them the next day in the workshop. In any case, why should I have chosen a Jewish restaurant? Who wants a Jewish restaurant when he has everything he needs at home?

And now I began to understand why Mme Andrée was telling me this whole story about the war.

Her sister, whose name I forget, has written her a letter. And what does the little sister say in this letter? She says it's no life staying in a small town like Angers where everyone knows her; what she would really like is to come to Paris, where life must be more pleasant and where she doesn't know anyone except her big sister. She could work, like her sister, for a tailor; surely she could find a workshop where they needed a willing, hard-working girl. Mme Andrée is asking me to help.

Now, that is some favour she's asking! It's as welcome as a fall in orders at the height of the season. And suddenly I realize that I really am a schmuck, because I think I know now why Mme Andrée said yes to my invitation: 'Monsieur Albert's a real sucker: I've got to find my sister a job and here he is, inviting me out to dinner while his wife and children are away in Brussels. Anyone else would have taken advantage of it to ask for a rise, but I'm going to get a position for my baby sister who went and got her head shaved.'

What on earth can these sisters be thinking? That her hair has grown again and the war is forgotten? You go to the hairdresser, have a perm and there you are: 'La-de-da, sit on a cushion and sew a fine seam'?

I'm just looking up to say that it can't be done, that I can't do it, I could never do it, without the shame falling on to me. I couldn't do it in spite of time, which rolls on and sometimes helps us to forget. But who does forget? Instead I don't say a thing. I don't say anything because Maria Montez's eyes are still full of tears and also full of innocence. What I want now is to take her hands. Stop! Remove your hand! Are you mad? I look at my hands: they haven't budged. Albert, why don't you get on with your meal? How is the meat? Like meat. So? So the air from my lungs is stuck in my throat and is stopping anything from going down, and the meal is ruined.

There you have it. You try to spend a nice quiet evening, because life doesn't last a hundred years, and then a letter arrives from Angers, and I have to be the one who gets the good news.

Well, we wished one another good night and said, See you in the morning, and she went off in one direction and I in another.

On the other side of the boulevard people were standing on the pavement listening to a small band in a café playing a song by Pierre Dudan. On my way home I took a short cut through the Rue Béranger and there, perhaps because I felt better, I started to whistle.

I stood at the door of the flat for a while, trying to think what it was I had been whistling in the street. Just as I was putting the key in the door, the lights on the stairway went out and that was when I remembered the words of the song:

Life tells me a tale
Of sin and love and chastisement;
And sometimes life tells
*A tale without an ending.**

I turned on the light and went in.

The next day Léa came back with the children and some Belgian chocolate. In bed that night, she told me about her trip. She talked about those who were missing and about those who were still there. A little while later, it was like it was at the Liberation, when we had been apart for too long.

*Poem by Louis Miller, translated from the Yiddish by Charles Dobzinski.

'Hush, hush! Léon is acting'

'Don't breathe, don't breathe . . . You must realize how serious it is . . . Your heart . . .'

Léon's ear was pressed to the chest of the dummy which had been placed in the centre of the workshop so that we could see it better; then, very quickly, he slipped behind it. Only his head was visible above the latest model from Wasserman's that he had just ironed.

'You mean, it's a Jewish heart?'

'Yes, you could call it that: a Jewish heart.' (Léon had gone back to holding his ear pressed to the heart of the dummy.)

'I, myself, whom you see before you, I, too, have a sick heart . . .' Léon drew himself up and held the dummy against his own chest, but not for long, because he had to deliver its next line.

'You, too? What do you expect . . . A Jewish heart sometimes races like a horse and sometimes goes at a snail's pace. But in spite of everything, I can tell you it's a heart of iron, because what this heart has seen . . .'

'Haven't you had some treatment for it? Didn't you do anything?'

'What do you mean, "do anything"? If you only knew how many doctors I've seen. They all say that the best cure for my heart is peace and quiet. Calm, doctor! I need calm! No stress, no worries, just calm. But try asking a doctor to give you a prescription for calm in this life!'

Léon acted with the avant-garde Jewish theatre, the PYAT. Every time he was in a new play, you could be sure that he would act it out the next day at work.

It was a long time since he had made his début on the stage. In 1931, when he was ten, Léon came to Paris to look for his elder brother. But all he knew of his brother was his name. His mother, who stayed behind in Przytyk, in Poland, had given him nothing except a few things packed into a suitcase. When he got off the train at the Gare de l'Est, he naturally followed the Boulevard Magenta towards the Place de la République. He was looking right and left as he reached the Rue de Lancry, when he spotted a notice announcing a performance by the Yiddish Theatre. He waited there, sitting on his case, and struck up a conversation with the first person who stopped to read the poster. With his suitcase on the ground and his big cap on his head, it was no surprise when Léon opened his mouth and spoke Yiddish. Five minutes later he was at the Jewish Cultural League, which just happened to have its premises at number 10, Rue de Lancry. And that's how he found the address of his brother and became acquainted with the Yiddish Theatre, which was already being run by Kinman, the author of *La Réforme*, the play that Léon was appearing in last night.

Léon had two heroes: Maurice Schwartz and Raimu.

Maurice Schwartz came to Paris in 1938 with his company from the Yiddish Theater in New York. It was the topic of conversation for weeks afterwards. And today Léon again put his iron down to tell us about Maurice Schwartz in *Tevy the Dairyman*.

'At one point in the play,' Léon explained, 'old Tevy is going to the station with Hodel, one of his daughters. He is going with her because she is off to join her fiancé, who was deported to Siberia by the Tsar. At the station Tevy clasps his daughter in his arms and embraces her. And as he kisses her, we know that he is seeing little Hodel for the last time. Then suddenly, Maurice Schwartz, who was playing Tevy, turned to the audience and spoke this famous line: "Do you know what, Reb Sholem Aleichem: we'd rather talk about something pleasant: what news of the war?"

'Do you think he was crying, Maurice Schwartz? No, we were the ones who were crying! All around the Théâtre de la Porte Saint-Martin, you could hear people blowing their noses. That's theatre! Apart from Raimu, there isn't another actor who could do that.'

'Raimu is no great actor,' Mme Paulette said.

Léon had picked up his iron. Now he put it down again.

'You know something about Raimu, do you? Have you ever seen Raimu? *La Femme du boulanger*? Did you see him in *La Femme du boulanger*?'

'Yes, I've seen that play.'

'Madame Paulette,' Léon said, 'for the hundredth time: in the cinema, you don't see plays, you see films. All the time, you talk about plays! You see plays in the theatre, not in the cinema. Anyway, people talk about a *stage* play, but not a cinema play. In the theatre, the actors are there on the stage and, if it was allowed, you could get up and touch them. Why can't you touch the actors in the cinema, Madame Paulette? Because in the cinema there is a projector at the back of the house which sends pictures on to a white screen, and if we should ever want to get up and touch the actors, not only is it not allowed there either, but the only thing our fingers would touch is cloth. But would you like to know what the cinema's good for? For the memory. When an actor dies, his films remain. And our children and our children's children can go and see *La Femme du boulanger* and they will still know that Raimu was the greatest actor of them all.'

'With that accent of his, that Raimu, he can't be a good actor,' Mme Paulette persisted.

'Madame Paulette,' Léon answered, with no less persistence, 'am I telling you that with that accent of yours you can't be a good seamstress? Don't get upset, that's not what I'm saying. I'm not saying it, because it is beside the point. But with Raimu, yes, it is the point. It's the point because his accent is true, and an actor who doesn't possess the truth can walk on his hands or climb on the ceiling, but he will never be a great actor. How can I explain it? If you don't go to the cinema to see *La Femme du boulanger*, which is a *film*, it doesn't matter; no one will tell Raimu. But if you want to see a play, a real play, go to the theatre. They knock three times,* the curtain goes up and the performance begins. Well, in theory at least.'

Léon said 'in theory' because his own experience as an actor at the Yiddish Theatre had taught him, among other things, that neither the three knocks, nor the curtain rising – and not even the speaking of the first lines – were any guarantee that the play had really begun; naturally, in spite of the opening lines, the members of the audience carry on with their conversations, and if somebody (I mean, an outsider) were to come into the

---

*In France the stage manager knocks three times with his baton when the play is about to begin (translator's note).

theatre at that moment, he might well assume that some people had to explain what was going on to their neighbours who didn't understand Yiddish, or else that they were commenting on the set or the costumes. But if the outsider understood Yiddish, he would soon realize that the subject of discussion was usually nothing to do with the play; indeed he might wonder why the spectacle on the stage was determined to get started when the one in the auditorium had not yet ended. This is why Léon says that the real competition faced by the Yiddish Theatre does not come from other theatres, but from the audience.

However, the worst thing of all is when some people start to say, 'Hush, hush!' – usually relatives of the actors. Then the debates and arguments swell to such a pitch that the actors have to stop playing and only after cries of 'We're free now! The war is over! I've paid for my seat!' or else 'My son, he was in the Resistance!' can the performance really begin.

One day – it was the first play they put on after the Liberation – an actor decided to be clever. He clapped his hands, turned to the audience and, hoping to make them shut up, shouted: '*Yiden! Abi me zeyt zech!*'* He was right: *Abi me zeyt zech!* It was true that the Jews were there above all to meet one another. The whole audience

---

*'Jews! The main thing is for us to meet!'

applauded and every one of them started to talk and move around the rows of seats, because they were so happy to see one another. That evening, because there was an interval as well, anyone who didn't live nearby had to take a taxi home.

Léon once said: 'The cinema is a dream and the theatre is the human condition.' We all stared, because we're not used to hearing things in the workshop which you don't normally find outside books. But it gave us something to think about. As far as the cinema is concerned, he was right. With Maria Montez, Simone Simon and Danielle Darrieux, you could dream for years. But it was harder to understand about the theatre. The human condition? It's true that there have always been people who will pay good money to see a tragedy on the stage. They say that with the Greeks that's already how it was.

So, now I'm wondering: why is it that Léon earns his living at the ironing table? Because he is not paid for acting at the PYAT any more than he is for acting at work. It's not a job, being a Jewish actor, and the slack season lasts a good deal longer in the Yiddish Theatre than it does in the rag trade. Who can fill the Yiddish Theatre after the first few performances?

Perhaps it was the auditorium Léon was referring to when he said that the theatre is the human condition.

A Simple Matter of
Common Sense

'So Léon,' M. Albert asked me, 'when's the Bris?'

'The doctor says, in about two weeks' time.'

'Bris?' said Jacqueline. 'What's the Bris?'

I explained to her (because she always wants to know everything) that it was circumcision and that it took place traditionally a week after the child's birth.

'And what if it's a girl?'

'If it's a girl, that won't stop me saying *mazel tov** and coming to work with a cake and a bottle of slivovitz.'

'So all Jews are circumcised, are they?' Jacqueline went on, still curious.

'It depends on the parents, but generally, yes, you could say that all Jewish boys are circumcised.'

'But it must hurt them!'

'I really don't remember. But you know, Jacqueline,

*'Good luck'. Used especially at weddings, births, etc.

that's the greatest pain I would wish on a child. When a child falls over or cuts himself and it bleeds, you put a plaster on, give him a sweet and he stops crying. This is the same: you put a dressing on, the mother gives him his milk and so he stops crying.'

'But who does it?' Mme Andrée asked.

'Nowadays, it's done more and more in hospital, but usually it's still a *mohel*, who is a sort of rabbi, but who specializes in circumcisions.'

'And what happened during the war?' Mme Andrée asked.

'Generally, I can't say. As far as my son is concerned, it went very well. The *mohel* came to the neighbour's who had taken us in. Sammy was born on 10 July 1942, which was six days before the round-up at the Vel' d'Hiv.* The circumcision took place ten days later, because it was dangerous for a Jew to walk around in Paris, especially for the *mohel*, who had a beard that you could see from even further away than a yellow star on a jacket.'

'Are you crazy, or what?' Jacqueline burst out angrily. 'Since that's how they recognize Jewish boys, whatever made you have him circumcised? I don't know . . . It was . . . it was suicide . . . I don't get it.'

---

*The sports stadium used as an assembly point during the mass deportation of Jews in 1942 (translator's note).

'Quite so,' I said. 'It was precisely because we didn't know what would become of him that he had to be made a Jew as soon as possible.'

I would like to have explained it to her better than that, but it was complicated. I would need to explain that it was something like an act of defiance, that for me it was the same when a little while later I joined the Resistance with the UJJ.* I would have to explain that it was precisely because there was a danger of the child dying that the *mohel* wanted to carry out the operation that would make him a Jew. And because there was that danger, I wanted Sammy's life, however short it might be, to be the life of a Jew.

But, of course, all that was complicated, so I didn't say it. I merely said, 'You know, I've never been ashamed of being a Jew, myself!'

I noticed that M. Albert had raised his eyes to see if I was looking at Mme Paulette. He saw that I was.

After that there was a short silence before Mme Andrée asked me about the extra work that Fanny would have with another child.

'We've decided to put Sammy in infant school.'

'Has anyone told him?' Charles asked, even though he never takes part in these discussions.

***Union de la Jeunesse Juive*: the Jewish Youth Union.

'Of course we have,' I answered. 'We explained that he is grown up now and that all children of his age are already at school. And since he's intelligent, he understood right away.'

'Grown up! Does anyone tell a child that he's grown up? No one tells a child that he's grown up! A child is never grown up! A child is a child! What has intelligence got to do with a child, who doesn't even know what intelligence is? There's only one thing that a child knows: that he doesn't want to grow up, and that his father and mother are looking after him, and no one else!'

'But, Charles, a child has to learn things like responsibility. When I was four . . .'

'*Toi!*' – it was the first time Charles had used the familiar form to me. 'When you were four you had a big brother and big sisters. A child is not responsible, because he doesn't want to be responsible! The only responsible people are his mother and father. Does your son wet his bed, Léon? No? Good. But you should be ready to change his sheets in the morning, even so. What does it mean: grown up? *Yingele,** you must go to school like a grown up to learn to read like a grown up. You will eat your meat like a grown up. You will tie your shoelaces like a grown up and wipe your bottom

---

*Affectionate term in Yiddish for a small boy.

like a grown up and while you are at school getting more intelligent, your little sister will stay at home and drink all your mama's milk and Mama will be tired. So you must be sensible, because Mama can't take care of you any more ... Don't you see? Can't look after ...'

He suddenly stopped. It was as though the furrows had deepened on his face, like two paths designed to carry away the tears. But Charles didn't cry, he merely went back to his sewing machine.

I don't know anything better than work for taking your mind off things.

Everyone agrees on that score. What was it they wrote above the entrance to the camps? '*Arbeit macht frei.*' In French, they say that work means health, and you could roughly translate the Yiddish saying on the subject as 'The hardest work is not to have any'.

In any case, if by any chance I should wonder what to talk to Fanny about this evening, Charles has given me a good topic of conversation. But, as for saying that it's the kind of conversation I enjoy having with Charles, that you couldn't.

One day Betty was hanging around the shop with a slice of bread, as she often does after school; she had just come back from holiday camp, so Jacqueline asked her to sing one of the songs they had taught her there.

Of course, at the C C E* they weren't going to teach the children the songs of Tino Rossi, so Betty sang in Yiddish:

> *Es hot di kleyne Tsipelè*
> *Farbisn zich a lipelè*
> *—Tsipelè, vos veynstu?*
> *An apelè, dos meynstu?*
> *—Neyn, neyn, neyn,*
> *Ver zogt dos, az ich veyn?†*

While she was singing, Betty leant against her father's sewing machine, not far from Charles, who, together with Maurice, had stopped his machine so as not to make any noise. In fact, apart from Mme Paulette, of course, everyone in the shop had stopped work. As for M. Albert, he was trying to mark out a garment on several layers of cloth, but that was mainly to keep his hands busy: and by the way they shook, you could see that the scrap of a thing who was singing was the apple of his eye.

When the song was over, Charles wiped his glasses,

Commission Centrale de l'Enfance: Central Committee for Children, set up before the Liberation by the Jewish Union for Resistance and Mutual Aid (*Union des Juifs pour la Résistance et l'Entreaide*), mainly to save the lives of Jewish children.

†Once little Tsipele/ Bit her little lip/ 'Why are you crying, Tsipele?/ Is it an apple you want?'/ 'No, no, no/ Who dares say I'm crying?'

as he often did, and then reached out a hand towards Betty. He stroked – no, not stroked – he just touched the lock of blond hair on her shoulder with the tips of his fingers. At that moment Mme Andrée's face went as white as the snow in Poland. Whereupon I started to clap. I clapped because it was the best thing to do, and the others joined in with the clapping, because it was the best thing to do. Jacqueline asked what the words meant and, as Betty didn't know, I translated for her. 'How pretty,' Jacqueline said, and kissed Betty.

Pretty? Of course, it was. There's nothing I know of – apart from the songs of Renée Lebas – as beautiful as a song in Yiddish. It's beautiful and often sad – and perhaps that's why it's beautiful.

In fact at the Yiddish Theatre, as soon as they start to sing on the stage, people in the audience begin to cry. Not only, as you might think, because of the words, although there is a whole repertoire of sad songs in Yiddish: no, as soon as the first words are sung, the handkerchiefs start coming out of the handbags. Anyhow, I won't try to explain.

You could say that the workshop is rather like a theatre, though with this difference: in the shop we are all on stage, playing the same part in the same play, and we don't need any rehearsals before we go on.

At the Yiddish Theatre, the only time I also appear in a workshop is in Sholem Aleichem's *The Big Prize*, except that then I'm not a presser, as I am here; I play the part of Motel, one of the two apprentices. I used to play Motel before the war, and then, as they couldn't find a boy who knew Yiddish well enough to act the part, I went back to it. It's not important, anyhow, because the words Sholem Aleichem writes just need to be spoken, that's all.

After Jacqueline had kissed her, Betty naturally went round the whole shop offering her cheek.

'Very well, now go and do your homework,' M. Albert said, bustling her towards the kitchen, because silence had fallen over the shop. It wasn't one of those silences that falls after a big argument and it wasn't one of those that happen in peak periods when no one is talking simply because everyone has too much to do. No, it was just one of those silences that fall from time to time nowadays in tailors' shops.

We could have done with a visit from Isy the rag-and-bone man, Madame Léa's brother. You can hear him every time behind the door: 'Listen! Listen to this!' And as soon as he comes into the room he is telling us the latest story by Roger Nicolas, even before saying hello. But we were not likely to see him that day, because it's usually in the mornings that he comes schnorring* round the courtyards, as M. Albert says.

*schnorr: beg, ask for alms.

I was waiting for Jacqueline to say something, because she is often the one who manages to save an awkward situation, by talking about this or that. On this occasion, she just hummed. Then it occurred to me that if Jacqueline couldn't find anything to take our minds off what we were thinking, perhaps it was because she was wondering if it had been such a good idea after all to ask Betty to sing. Then I recognized Charles Trenet's 'Romance de Paris' and I started to whistle it myself, at first softly, then more loudly so that the others could hear me, and Jacqueline also began to hum louder; when it comes down to it, apart from work, there's nothing better than singing, when the words are too hard to say.

Coming back to the question we started with – I mean the discussion about circumcision – I thought for a time that Jacqueline had something more she wanted to ask, because I saw her hand pause from time to time between two points. But the question came from Mme Andrée:

'Monsieur Léon, why did you want to have a child when there was a war on?'

'Why did we want one? Did we really want one? . . . You know very well, Madame Andrée, that the best recipe not to have children is usually to have separate rooms. At one time, with Fanny and me, though this was after the boy was born, we even had separate towns, which naturally cut down on the risks. Otherwise, it's a matter of common sense.'

'Common sense?' said Jacqueline, in astonishment. 'What has common sense got to do with it?'

'I'll tell you, Jacqueline. When Fanny got pregnant, her father was furious. Not because we weren't married, but for the very reason that Jews had already been sent to the camps at Pithiviers and Beaune-la-Rolande. And also to Drancy. Yet I remember, when Fanny and I told her parents the news, we were very proud and held hands like they do on those notices you can see right now on the walls. At first, her father said nothing, because of course he was not someone who was in the habit of talking about such things. Then he started to walk up and down, and suddenly he came to a halt opposite me and said: "Léon, all my life, when I've wanted to go to République, I've got out at Oberkampf!"* There you are, Jacqueline, getting out at Oberkampf – that's common sense.'

---

*On the Paris metro, the station before République (translator's note).

Our Children's Future

You can never learn early enough to use your wits.

The other day a delivery man came into the courtyard with a large parcel on his back. I could see him through the window behind my cutting table. It was only when he put down the parcel that you could see there was a delivery man underneath it. He took his cap off, to wipe his forehead, as I thought, but then from his head, on which there wasn't a hair left, he removed a piece of paper. There was a name on it, my name. I know, because shortly after that he rang the bell. He was bringing the linings from Wasserman's. When I saw him struggling to pick up the parcel again I thought to myself: he should have made a note of my name not on his head, but in it. But there must have been some wrinkles in that head which made it impossible to note down names. And that's the kind of wrinkle that can't be got rid of by running an iron over it.

It's not something you can say about Joseph, the one

who took over for a while from Léon as the presser: he has no wrinkles in his head. He would make wrinkles, usually where they weren't needed, on the clothes. Which is why as a presser he would have time on his hands even at the height of the season. As I've always thought, you can't be studying and in the workshop at the same time.

Joseph still comes to the house every week to teach Raphaël. Not that Raphaël really needs the lessons, but when Léon came back to work, Léa and I didn't have the heart to dismiss Joseph outright, even though we had told him from the start that the post was temporary.

'Hello-hello' was the first to mention him, saying that he had his *baccalauréat*. But it was when she told Léa that his parents were deportees that we agreed to try him out. After all, who needs a scholar at an ironing table? Joseph was what you'd call a real scholar.

To give you one example: once, Mme Sarah sold a couple of bars of soap in the shop and came as usual to say 'hello-hello' to Léa in the kitchen. As it was very hot that day, instead of the usual glass of tea, Léa offered her a glass of beer. She drank down the beer in one go, without drawing breath, because, as I said, it was very hot. And then, after putting her glass down on the table, as if ashamed of her enjoyment, she said in Yiddish: 'Piss!'

The beer may not have been cold enough, but, even so, this was not very polite, and ever since then Léa has only offered her tea.

Joseph laughed when he heard the story, and explained why.

'I believe that, since her husband was deported, Madame Sarah has made up her mind once and for all that she will no longer enjoy anything in life. To her, saying that something is good would mean accepting the notion that life has returned to normal, with some things that are good and others not so good. And then, there could be something else. The things that Madame Sarah and her husband enjoyed were things they enjoyed together. You can be sure that she never tasted anything without sharing it with her husband. So when she said that the beer tasted bad, it wasn't out of malice, or hypocrisy towards herself, even if the beer was fine. I just think that for her things will always have a taste of bitterness.'

I thought at once that it was not the lessons Joseph was giving Raphaël that would make an idiot of the boy. We could even start planning a fine future for him. And what can parents do better than to plan for their children's future?

Léa would like Raphaël to become an artist, but I don't agree. Not that Raphaël isn't good at drawing, quite the opposite. When he was only eleven, he did a painting of the fable about the Fox and the Crow. You saw the Crow twice: once in the tree, and then in a lake, but back to front, because what you saw in the lake was the reflection. You should have seen the lake he painted: a person could see himself in it. No, my objection to him becoming an artist is because it is an uncertain future. It's not a future with good prospects, because generally when you hear people talk about a painter, it's because he's dead already. And before he dies, he spends his life as a *schnorrer*.

Last week M. Schiffman, the one who sold us the subscription to *Droit et Liberté* and who also does the collection for the charity fête, came to the shop to sell some paintings by Jewish artists. But the discussion got off to a bad start because he launched into his spiel by saying that it was a good investment.

'Why are you talking about investment?' I asked him. 'Don't you think I can buy a picture just because I like it?'

'I'm talking about investment because, alas, when they are alive, painters sell very few works, yet often after they are dead their pictures are worth an absolute fortune.'

'Very well. Then please explain something to me, Monsieur Schiffman: why do painters not make pictures which sell when they are alive? Do I make clothes that will only sell when I'm dead?'

'Because,' he told me, 'on the whole artists are ahead of their time and people at the time are not always able to appreciate what they are doing.'

'So explain something else: if these artists of yours are so clever, why don't they do some pictures ahead of their time, and once in a while a picture right on time, which would allow them to live?'

'Just so. I have here some pictures which are right on time, as you say.'

'Do you think I'm an idiot, Monsieur Schiffman? A moment ago you were speaking about pictures that one day would be worth a fortune, and you want to sell me a picture with no future?'

I took advantage of the time it took M. Schiffman to find an answer to that to ask him why painters needed a salesman, especially one who was surely not getting any commission.

'When a painter paints,' he said, 'he paints. He doesn't bother about sales.'

'Why? Is he building up his stock? Has he no one to advise him? Don't artists know how to keep accounts? Do you know what you should do, Monsieur Schiffman? You . . .'

'I know very well what to do, Monsieur Albert. What do you imagine: that an artist needs our advice or our pity? An artist does what it is his duty to do and it is the duty of a people like ours to encourage its artists.

Look closely at these pictures, Monsieur Albert: they are signed Szrajer, Kirszenbaum, Glatzer, Borvine-Frenkel. And look at what's in them: they describe something that you won't see again. You won't see it again because it no longer exists. And if one day your children want to know what a Jew's life was like in Poland, they may perhaps learn it from you if you still feel like talking about it. But they will learn more thanks to artists whose talent enables them to speak to us of the past. It's not a Picasso that I'm asking you to buy, and not only because you wouldn't be able to afford it . . .'

'Why? Is he expensive, Picasso?'

'Just how much, I can't tell you. Perhaps . . . ten million.'

'Ten million?'

Since painters are paid piece-work, I immediately began to wonder how many pictures Picasso could do in a month.

In the end, of course, I bought a picture. Before that, M. Schiffman also told me that I could have one in exchange for a suit. But I didn't want to do that. I didn't want to not just because at the height of the season I never have time to make a man's suit to measure, but also because it embarrassed me. I preferred to pay, and I chose a painting by Borvine-Frenkel. It shows a Jew running through the snow carrying a double bass on his back like a child that has grown up too fast. There is a village in the distance, but he has his back turned to it.

For an extra two hundred francs I also became a member of 'Friends of Jewish Artists', even though I was really cross. I was cross because from the start I knew that I would buy a picture, and on top of that I would have to explain to Léa that I'd got a bargain.

But Léa didn't complain. She even said that the picture would make a good model for Raphaël to copy and we hung it in the dining room. As a result, if I ever considered trying to forget what a *shtetl** looked like, I wouldn't be able to.

So far, Raphaël hasn't made a copy of the picture. Léa thinks that when he does, no one will be able to say which was copied from the other.

The same evening that we put up the picture, we talked about the children's future. Especially about Raphaël's, because he's a boy. I was reading the newspaper, even though Léa doesn't like me to read it in bed, but I can't sleep until I know what's going on in the world.

'One must face facts,' Léa said. 'Raphaël is an artist.'

*Village with a large Jewish population, in Eastern Europe.

'One can face facts and still have a good job. There's no law against that.'

'Do you want him to be a tailor, like you?'

'For you, it's got to be either artist or tailor!'

'No,' Léa replied. 'What I want for my children is for them to be happy.'

'Precisely,' I said. 'For children to be happy, they must have a good job. Especially a boy.'

By the time we turned out the light, Raphaël had earned a living in so many professions that it would have taken him two lifetimes to learn them all.

'I think there was once a painter called Raphaël already,' Léa said after a moment's silence.

'Do you want to start again? What do I know about it, and what difference does it make?'

'The difference,' said Léa, 'is that it might bring him luck. We can find out by looking in the children's dictionary.'

I knew that the discussion would not come to an end nor move on until I had gone to look in the dictionary, so I got up. I didn't put the light on in the children's room, so as not to wake them, but in the light coming from the corridor, I could see by the expressions on their faces that neither Betty nor Raphaël was worrying about their future.

I put Betty's foot, which was sticking out, back under the blanket; she turned over and I took advantage of that to give her a kiss. And to say to her, quietly enough not to wake her, but loud enough for her to hear: '*Schlouf, maydele.*'*

I waited until her breathing was as calm as Raphaël's before going to find the dictionary, and looked at it in the kitchen over a glass of water.

'This Raphaël of yours, he died when he was thirty-seven,' I told Léa as I got back into bed. 'A piece of luck like that can stay in the dictionary. Now, since tomorrow morning isn't the deadline for taking a decision, we'll go to sleep, if you don't mind. That way you can perhaps have some ordinary dreams, instead of dreams that overflow into daytime. So, good night!'

It would not be altogether true to say that I went quickly to sleep, because I went on debating with Léa in my head. These are the best kinds of argument, because when you are wrong, you are the only one to know. Naturally, you calm down bit by bit, and that's when you really start to think.

To think seriously about what? Who was I really thinking about? The children, of course, and the future we dream of for them . . . Joseph, who is looking after his own future by himself . . . The Jewish musician running through the snow . . . Why is he all alone? Where are the others? The villagers? The village . . . We

*'Sleep, little girl.'

didn't even write. Just at Rosh-Hashana* and when the children were born . . . Perhaps the children would ask questions now, with the picture hanging in the dining room. But how could we answer them? When we light the candles for Yortzeit,† they look on and say nothing. We do things without explaining what we do.

'Are you asleep?' I asked Léa.

'No,' she said. 'What are you thinking about?'

'I'm thinking it's late,' I replied. 'And that tomorrow morning we have to deliver the work to Wasserman's.'

---

*New Year.
†Anniversary of a death.

'Thank You, Officer!'

There are some truths you can't keep on denying.

Imagine you are about to drink a glass of tea and you spill it on the table: people will think you are just clumsy. Now imagine that you spill this same glass of tea, not on the table, but on your trousers, and that the tea, moreover, is boiling hot. In that case you are a *shlimazl*.

I am a *shlimazl*. I have known it since the day I set foot in a workshop; or, to be more precise, since I set foot in a workshop to work there. Right away they sat me down at a machine, a Singer 31 K 15, to make an under-machinist out of me. An under-machinist is the one who sews the linings, makes up the back and the sleeves, and prepares the collar and the pocket flaps, while the machinist himself makes up the whole garment. That's why, as it happens, the machinist is paid piece-work, while the under-machinist is only paid by the week.

In a shop, while learning to sew, you also learn to save time. So, for example, when you make up the linings, first you put all the sleeves together, then all the backs, then the fronts with the backs. And, still out of a desire to save time, and because it's more practical, you leave each pair of sleeves joined by a thread.

On the Monday after I got my first pay, I thought it would be clever, in order to save effort, to hang the sleeves of the linings on the electric fitment right above my sewing machine. When they put the lights on towards the end of the afternoon, I didn't realize straightaway that the lighting was not as good as usual, and I went on with my under-machinist's job as usual.

All of a sudden, the shop was lit up, particularly above my head. I looked up, because at first I thought the voltage had changed: the heat from the lamp had heated up the metal shade and scorched the linings – and the light was coming through the holes. I glanced towards the boss: the brilliant light now shining in the room found no corresponding gleam in his face. For a short time he did not react, then, sadly, he just said, 'Joseph, *ziz mir finster far di oygn*.'* After that, as I didn't dare move, he said, more or less, 'What's the matter? You burn the linings and you think the work is done? That's what we mean by apprenticeship, Joseph. It's like life.

*'Joseph, it's gone dark in front of my eyes.'

84

There's a silly mistake you won't make next time. But, unfortunately for me, you'll make others.'

He was right.

Generally each of us cleans out his sewing machine at the end of the week, particularly the pieces round the spool, because that's where the dust and small bits of material gather. So you lift up the head of the machine and rest it against a kind of wooden wedge, which you put just behind it.

So why was there no wedge the day when, with the best will in the world, I lifted the head of my machine to clean it? I'll never know. Under its own weight, before I could do anything to catch it, the head of the machine toppled over the far side of the table and fell to the floor.

Once again, my boss at first stayed very quiet. But for longer than the first time, because a 31 K 15 is not as easy to replace as some sleeve linings.

And, once again, I didn't dare move. I was wondering who would be the first to faint: him or me. Just when I thought he was finally going to say something, someone began knocking loudly on the door.

'It's the anti-Semite from downstairs,' my boss said.

This is how he referred to our downstairs neighbour, because one day he overheard him saying that the house had been a lot quieter 'before'.

The anti-Semite's visit was good luck for me, because he got the benefit of my boss's wrath.

Since it's best to be paid piece-work, when I went to the next workshop I introduced myself as a full machinist. But the very first evening, after taking a look at my work, the boss took me aside. 'Right,' he said, 'you can put the garments together, but let me make up the collar and sleeves.' Then he set my rate of pay and for a few weeks everything went as we had agreed. Then came the day when my boss, M. Zaidman, who was hanging a garment on the dummy, coughed and said simply, 'You know, Joseph, even at the busiest time of year, women still button their coats on the same side.'

To see what he meant, I went to take a look at the coat on the dummy. I had put the three trimmed buttonholes on the wrong side.

'Can we darn it?' I asked.

He looked at me without answering. It gave me the chance to observe that my stupid mistakes, which ought to have provoked outbursts of anger, generally left my bosses rather quiet. It's not that they are at a loss for words. They just don't say them.

So, respecting M. Zaidman's silence, I didn't press the point. And yet it seemed to me that the buttonholes I had made were where they had been marked.

I went to the supplier to get another length of cloth

to replace the front of the coat, unable to understand how I had made the mistake. The answer came unexpectedly. I shall have to explain.

When a garment is cut, the cutter always marks the position of the tucks, pockets and buttonholes. But it can happen that, if he puts part of one garment on top of another, the chalk comes off on the second piece. Unfortunately, that is something I only realized the day when, for the very same reason, I made a pocket in the back of a coat.

You had to look at the situation from M. Zaidman's point of view, and, since I couldn't count on his patience for ever, I decided to become a presser. So it was that one day, thanks to Mme Sarah, I ended up at M. Albert's.

What happened immediately after that, up to the time of Léon's return, you know already. 'In this life, you have to keep your eyes open,' M. Albert told me one evening in his kitchen. So after mentally going over all my experiences at work, I came to an agreement with him and gave Léon his position back.

At the same time, I also found out something of which I am now quite certain: among all the employees in the dressmaking trade, I am always the first to be informed when the slack season comes.

The reason I've told all these stories is because they precede another story, which is the one I really want to tell. A story which, even though it may seem to have little to do with what has gone before, is in fact closely related to it. Here it is.

To start with, there was a wish, a desire. Or, more precisely, a determination that I think amounted to a choice: my parents, when they left Poland, chose to live in France. This desire lay behind the decision that took me to the Rue du Mont-Cenis, to the *commissariat de police* for the 18th *arrondissement* in Paris (where I resided) in order, now that the war is over, to request French nationality – a status which, if my parents had enjoyed it on 16 July 1942, might perhaps have kept them out of the hands of the Vichy police.

All well and good, except that the police officer, who had been a member of that same police force, tells me, after I fill in my application for naturalization, 'I can assure you that I shall do everything in my power to make certain that your request is not granted.'

It is 1946 and the police superintendent of the 18th *arrondissement*, the very same who arrested my parents in the Rue Marcadet, is telling me: 'I can assure you that I shall do everything in my power to make certain that your request is not granted.'

I look at him, at first without understanding what he has said, but he is already dealing with the next person in the queue. I look at him and I wonder what has changed, since he is still there, on the other side of the counter, and is still the police superintendent of the 18th *arrondissement*.

So I suddenly start talking to him in my head. I am talking to him because I need to understand, even though everything is muddled. Can you hear me, *Monsieur le commissaire*, I must talk to you. *Monsieur le commissaire*, you are the person who arrested my parents. Do you remember, Monsieur, it was on the morning of 16 July 1942 . . . Of course, you remember them, as you do all those whom you arrested that morning and piled into the buses going to the Vel' d'Hiv. What you don't know is that I escaped just before we got to the Vel' d'Hiv. I escaped and ran. A fourteen-year-old boy can run fast. He can run especially fast when he doesn't turn round to see his parents for one last time, because to do so would stop him from escaping. And, I'm sure of it now, my parents didn't look at me, either, so as not to attract attention to me. Courage, *Monsieur le commissaire*, that is real courage: not to look at one's child running away, in order to give him a chance to survive.

I ran without stopping once until I reached this 18th *arrondissement* of which you are still police super-intendent.

I'm talking to you, but you can't hear me, and I'm slowly walking towards the exit. Will they let me go? Will they arrest me? Of course not. No one cares about me. I'm of no interest to anyone. Everybody has his own problems to sort out with the officer. What about the policeman on the door: will he let me pass? Now, there's a funny thing: I automatically looked at the left-hand side of my chest. I smile and go past. There is some progress in the French police: nowadays they let Jews out of a police station. What have I to complain about? I'm standing on the pavement. If I want, I can cross the square, go into the café opposite and drink a glass of lemonade. They no longer have cafés where Jews and dogs are not allowed.

But I'm not going to cross the square or order a lemonade at the bar. On the contrary, I'm going back to rejoin the queue and wait my turn. I have to talk to you, *Monsieur le commissaire.* I have to tell you that you are giving me back my identity. Whether I like it or not, I am defined by your desire to put obstacles in the way of my request for naturalization. But you have to realize that that is more or less all you can do to me and, whether you like it or not, I shall be leaving this police station again in a few moments. I shall be leaving a free man. I shall be leaving stateless and free, and you will watch me go without understanding, and whatever you may think will have absolutely no importance whatsoever. But before I leave, I must tell you something. I must let you know something that I have just decided. I must communicate this decision to you because it is thanks to you that I suddenly have an overwhelming desire: the desire to write. Yes, *Monsieur le commissaire*, I shall write in order to become a writer. To become a writer in French. I'll give it whatever time it takes. I'll put whatever effort is necessary into it, but I shall write. No doubt I shall do a lot of other things as well, like continuing for some time to sell clothes which people other than myself have made, on Sunday mornings in the market at Kremlin-Bicêtre. I shall continue to give private lessons to make a living; but I shall write. I shall write in order to say what a scandal it is that you are here, in this police station, and to say that you have not managed to destroy everything, because I am alive, here, in front of you, with my plan to become a writer.

Now it's my turn again. Yes, *Monsieur le commissaire*, I'm back. You are looking at me in surprise: you don't understand. No, no, don't worry, you made yourself very clear just now. But it doesn't matter. You can repeat the sentence that I now know by heart; despite that I have come back to hear it again: 'I can assure you that I shall do everything in my power to make certain that your request is not granted.'

The trouble is, *Monsieur le commissaire*, that you are wrong. I haven't come back to ask you for anything. I shall not ask you for anything because I know now that what you did to me, that the thing you did, was not just a matter of carrying out orders. You did what you did because you don't like me. You don't like my name and you don't like me. I have come back, *Monsieur le commissaire*, just to say one thing to you: 'Thank you, *Monsieur le commissaire*.'

Präzisions-Uhren-Fabrik*

They are six or seven years old and have just gone back to bed after showing me some photos: little snapshots which they held out to me in turn, silently, but at the same time impatient almost to the point of pleading.

In most of the photos there is a gentleman standing next to a lady, who is generally smiling and carrying a child in her arms, almost a baby. On the back of the photos there is a date and sometimes a place name.

I had arrived that same morning as a teacher at the children's home. 'You'll see, Joseph,' Raphaël told me. 'It's a real château in huge grounds with statues and fountains. There's a tower at the top of the building where one's not allowed to go on one's own and from which you can see the Seine for several kilometres.

*Precision watch factory.

'And another thing, it's all very informal,' he added, and gave me a letter for his friend Georges.

In the home were 125 children of deportees.

I was welcomed by Mireille, one of the counsellors. It appeared that something unusual had just occurred which was worrying everyone, particularly Louba, the director. It was arranged that that same evening I should be solely responsible for putting to bed the five little boys who slept in the round room. So, in order that they should get to know me, Mireille invited me to spend the day with her, because she happened to be in charge of the youngest children.

During the afternoon, as I was trying to extract some jam from a large tin with a soup spoon, and succeeding better than I expected in spreading it on some slices of bread for their tea, Mireille told me that Maurice, the child who ran away just as I arrived, had been found, that things like that happened and that often it was the same ones who ran away.

I was sitting on the edge of David's bed. He had not shown me a photo. However, when the others went back to their own beds, I suddenly noticed that his arm was reaching out towards me. Hanging from a chain firmly clasped in his fist was a fob watch, swinging gently from side to side. The gesture and David's expression betrayed a sort of quiet obstinacy which instantly told me how deeply attached he was to the object dangling from his hand.

I motioned towards it.

'Is that your watch? Can I see it?'

David said nothing, but at the end of his outstretched arm – which seemed to wish to convey something to me and at the same time keep it secret – I saw the chain vanishing into a fold of his chubby little hand.

For a moment I was not sure what to do. Then I leant forward, my hands clasping the side of the bed so that I could put my ear as close as possible to the watch. David's companions looked at me in silence.

'It works well,' I said after a short time.

David gave a little smile.

Gaining confidence, I asked him if I could read what was written on the dial. David's arm did not move, so I read:

GLASHÜTTER
Präzisions-Uhren-Fabrik

'And it's very beautiful as well,' I said.

Once more David gave a little smile.

I experienced a feeling of satisfaction and also of unease, because I seemed to be invading his privacy. So I said a few words about the following day, which we should be spending together, and got up. Reaching the door, I wished the five boys goodnight and then turned out the lights.

Almost immediately, I heard the sound of someone falling. I put the lights back on: David was lying motionless on the floor next to his bed. The others seemed to be waiting to see what I would do.

'What happened? How did you fall?'

'In the dark, I can't see my bed,' David said, very seriously. 'So I fall.'

David's calm manner put me on my guard and stopped me smiling. I helped him to get back into bed. You have to leave the little light on, said Maxime, his neighbour, pointing to a lamp hanging just above the door. I finished tucking David in and this time, as I went out, I was careful to 'leave the little light on' before turning off the one in the ceiling. Once again I wished them goodnight, and went down to the dining room.

In the huge entrance hall there was a wall newspaper. I stopped to glance at it. It had drawings: some children making a circle, resistance workers blowing up a train, another resistance worker being shot. It had articles, and remarks written like replies to questions, and signed:

'*Deportees are songs.*' *(Liliane, 7)*
'*Deportees are those who come back.*' *(Janine, 7)*

And then this letter from Marcel, nine years old, to his mother:

I'm sending you this short letter from a long way away in the hope that when you get back you will be glad to read it. I'll always remember when the policemen came to look for you. Fernande was in the country and Michel and I were with Mme Jeannette, and our aunt came to warn you, but it was too late, the policemen had already taken you away. I have been in a little village in the Sarthe, I was well and I thought of you when I was looking after the cows and the white goat. I kiss you from a long way away and hope that I will soon kiss you on your real cheek.

A few counsellors were sitting at a table in a corner of the refectory and enjoying a moment's break together. 'It's a tradition,' Mireille had explained to me. 'We meet every evening after the children have gone to bed. We eat, we talk – we have to have a break.'

Mireille had not yet come down from the dormitories that she looked after. It had been a hard day. I went outside for a stroll in the grounds. I sat down on one of the front steps.

In a little while I felt someone standing behind me.

'Can I join you?'

It was Louba.

She sat down beside me and we stayed in silence for a moment. Then she started to tell me about little Maurice, who had run away and been found again.

'Does he often run away?'

'It's not running away. He just goes somewhere to

97

feel something that he probably cannot experience here. When he has had enough, he comes back. Or rather, he arranges to be found not very far away.'

'Don't you say anything to him?'

'No.'

'But aren't you anxious?'

'Yes. Every time. I even shake with anxiety.'

We were silent for a short while, then Louba asked me how my first dormitory had gone. I told her about the photos, David's watch and falling out of bed, and the little light.

'We should have warned you about the little light,' she said. Then she told me the story of the five small boys.

'Lots of children here were with me already in Le Masgelier. Le Masgelier is a children's home in the Creuse opened at the start of the war by the OSE.* Most of the children, after a lot of negotiation, had successfully been got out of the camps at Gurs and Rivesaltes. Especially from Gurs. The French authorities had dumped thousands of refugees in these camps on the pretext that they were being kept under observa-

---

Oeuvre de secours aux enfants et protection de la santé des populations juives: an aid organization for Jewish children and the health of Jewish communities, founded in Russia in 1912. The French branch was set up in 1935.

tion. First there were Spanish republicans, later, Jews. Lots of Jews. They had been expelled from Germany. Most came from the region of Baden and the Palatinate, and, because they were foreign, they had been declared suspect: suspect and dangerous, even though there were old people and children among them, and they were nothing more than victims of Nazism . . . Conditions in the camp were appalling, which is why the parents didn't hesitate to put the children in our care when it became possible . . . In August '42 the deportations at Gurs began. That is why the last children whom we managed to get out of the camps were given some objects of value or souvenirs by their parents, like the photographs that they showed you. It's good that they showed you the photos. You must remember that, Joseph. It means that they trust you. You must never let them down . . . I saw David's father give him the watch. He was sitting on the ground and he took David on his knee. David was still little more than a baby. His father wrapped his arms round him, as though to protect him. I don't know what he said, but I saw him take the watch out of his pocket, then he took David's thumb and index finger in his own and together, slowly, they wound up the watch. Then he put the watch to David's ear . . . and I saw David smile . . .'

Louba paused in the story for a little while, then went on: 'After that, his papa put the watch in David's hand

99

and closed his fingers round it, then he wrapped the chain around his fist. Since that time, every evening, he has wound up the watch as his father showed him.'

For some time, I kept David's story to myself; then, perhaps in an attempt to retain everything that Louba had told me that first evening, before I forgot, I tried to write it down.

David's story has acquired its full weight for me now, because every evening, shortly before I leave the little light on for the night, he gets me to listen to the tick-tock of his watch. I do so carefully and never fail to show him, every time, how much I appreciate its perfect regularity.

I have tried to write it, giving the words back to Louba – even though I know that they may not be exactly her words, and even though I may have confused the order of events – because I am sure that I have not distorted the meaning.

'David was three years old when he saw his parents for the last time. It is hard to know if he still has a clear picture of what they looked like. But they had a brilliant idea when they gave him that watch. Its regular ticking, its hands showing the hours and the seconds, are something of them which continues to live and has been handed down to him, something he has received from them, and which he in turn has to make live. This is why every evening, without fail, David gives life again to that watch, as his father showed him. And this is also why, every morning, his first gesture is to bring it to his ear. What is important is not that the watch should tell the right time, but that it should never stop. I don't suppose I shall ever know how David, who could not count, has always known with absolute precision how to give the same number of turns to the winder. Even though he is very small, David vaguely realizes that he is responsible, despite the fact that the word doesn't yet mean much to him. He has no photograph of his parents, but the watch, which he guards so preciously, takes the place of a photograph for him.'

A few days later, unable to give shape to what Louba had told me, I drew up a list of a few words, for later use:

A trace.
A benchmark.
Continuity.
Reassuring presence.
A link.
The continuation.
Sharing.
Fidelity.
Tenacity.
Reassure, quieten, calm, soothe.

A few days after that, I recalled some other things that Louba had said and again wrote down:

'The children enjoy listening to each other's heartbeat. It's almost as though David were listening to his parents' heart each morning. He understood that his parents were in danger, that their hearts could no longer beat naturally, as his does, and that he must ensure that his precious watch continues to work properly. It's a terribly heavy responsibility for such a small child, having two lives that are so precious to him in his hands. This is why there is always a hint of sadness in David's smile. I cannot imagine how broken he would be if the watch were to be lost or even just to stop working. I should be very afraid for him the day that happened. And yet, despite it being such a heavy responsibility, I tell myself that the watch is David's great hope. When I try to find a precise image of happiness, I can see it in David's smile when he has his ear pressed to the watch, despite the sadness behind it, and even though I know that this happiness is fragile and under threat.' As we sat on the front step that first evening, Louba and I talked for a little longer. I asked her very few questions.

'Children,' Louba told me, 'especially small children, are inquisitive and receptive beings. A grasshopper's leap, an ant carrying a blade of grass, or the spots on the back of a ladybird are all that's needed to make them happy. Many children here have lost their relish for that inquisitiveness. We are here partly to help them discover it again.'

In answer to a question about David, she added:

'No, he doesn't rebel. He doesn't rebel because there is not yet any anger in him, only sorrow.'

I can't write down David's story. Not yet. I am simply recording what I remember and what I understand, because I don't understand it completely. (Though Louba told me: 'You, Joseph, you'll understand all these things very quickly.') Later, when I have the right words, I'll tell David's story. Perhaps one day, the words will put themselves in order of their own accord. But perhaps I shall never be able to write his story.

That first evening, I did just what Louba told me to do. Instead of putting the light on in the corridor leading to the round room, I found my way by the little light shining over the five sleeping boys. I leant over David's bed. He had slipped his right hand under his pillow, where it would soothe him through the night. On his cheeks were the traces of tears that had not yet dried.

Letter from Georges

Manoir de D.

Dear Raphaël,

I did get your last two letters safely — the one you gave Joseph and the one where you are surprised not to have had any reply.

I wanted to answer your first letter at once, but you know how it is, I put it off and in the meantime your second letter arrived.

I get on well with Joseph. He is in charge of the little ones, but as he is also responsible for looking after the library, where new books are constantly arriving, I see him a lot. I help him a little and he advises me what to read: Romain Rolland, Anatole France, Ilya Ehrenburg's The Fall of Paris. *Joseph is someone who never reads without a pencil in his hand. I have just started* Childhood *by Maxim Gorky. It's the story of a child whose father is dead, who is sent to his grandfather's family in Nizhni-Novgorod, by boat up the Volga.*

What I like is that the journey is well located geographically. The towns are named and given in chronological order: Astrakhan,

Saratov, Simbursk, Nizhni-Novgorod. Of course, the list is not complete in the book but I liked the names of the towns so much that when I read them I felt as though I had always known them by heart. I was sorry that there weren't more, so I completed the list with the help of a dictionary. I also noted that the Volga is the longest river in Europe (3,694 km), that it rises in the Valdaï plateau and that it passes through Kalinin, Iaroslavl, Kostroma, Gorki, Kazan, Ulyanovsk, Kuybychev, Saratov, Stalingrad and Astrakhan, before flowing into the Caspian Sea. I also learned that Nizhni-Novgorod was renamed Gorki in homage to the writer, who came from the town, and that it is quite common in the USSR to rename towns, usually after famous men. So, Stalingrad was once Tsaritsin, Kuybychev was called Samara, Iver became Kalinin, and Simbirsk, Ulyanovsk after Lenin's real name. The most remarkable of all must be St Petersburg, which was renamed Petrograd before being rechristened Leningrad.

When we next play 'I've been to',* that game I liked so much last summer, I'm going to try to stick to mentioning only Russian towns.

---

*'I've been to' is a memory game, played as follows: the players sit round in a circle. The first player says: 'I've been to . . .', followed by the name of a town. The next player says: 'I've been to . . .', followed by the first town, then another. And so on, until everyone has played. Any player who gets the order wrong or omits a town goes out. It usually takes several rounds before all the players are out. The winner, naturally, is the last person who can recite all the towns visited, in the correct order.

I also noticed that there are phrases or ideas in Childhood *that are repeated at intervals. One, which is a repeated feeling, struck me particularly. It comes back in a slightly different form a few pages apart. On page 19 (about the grandfather): 'I examined him with particular attention and an uneasy curiosity.' Then, a few pages later (after the child has been ill): 'From then on, I paid an uneasy attention to all human beings.'*

I suppose the same thing must occur in other books, but until now I hadn't noticed it.

Bit by bit, I have the feeling that a love of reading is becoming more and more important. It means that I can be alone with a story, in a corner of the grounds or in bed. What I like most of all is being able to stop, go back and re-read as often as I want. I think I still like the cinema, but I don't go often enough. Perhaps that is another reason why I enjoy reading so much.

Apart from that, the château nearly burned down.

Do you remember the Lipsztejn brothers? They are now seven and nine years old, but still the same little terrors. It was the younger one who nearly set fire to the place. He couldn't find one of his socks, so he crawled under his bed to look for it with a lighted candle (which he had found somewhere or other). Of course his horsehair mattress caught fire and Isidore, frightened that he would be told off, instead of calling for help, tried to put it out by blowing on it as hard as he could. Needless to say, that didn't help. Luckily Joseph was in the corridor and smelled the smoke, so he ran in with one of the fire extinguishers which they have hanging on the walls. Only when the bed was almost smothered in foam did he notice Isidore's legs sticking out from under the bed — Isidore still didn't dare to show himself. Joseph dragged him out by the legs while the extinguisher went on pouring foam into the whole room. The result was that the Isidore who emerged from beneath the bed was unrecognizable. When his brother saw him in that state, he shouted at Joseph, calling him an idiot and saying that if Isidore went blind because of him, he would make him pay a pension for his whole life, and lots of other things, until Louba stepped in and restored order.

A few days later Isidore was late for breakfast again. Joseph was just pouring the cocoa into the bowls for the little ones when Félix, the brother, who was eating breakfast at the next table, jumped up. He grabbed the butter knife and threatened the children: 'The first one to drink my brother's cocoa before he is sitting at the table will get this in his belly!' The children didn't have a chance to be frightened, nor Joseph to respond, because Isidore was just quietly coming into the dining room. As his responsible elder brother, Félix gave him one to teach him not to be late again. Isidore sheepishly took his seat, Joseph said, 'Eat up, children!' and Félix went back to his own place.

In spite of everything, Joseph is very fond of the Lipsztejn brothers. He tells me that he is more reassured by their feelings for one another than he is worried by the disasters they may cause.

One last thing about Isidore: yesterday he came to the library to borrow a book which, because of the quality of the illustrations, ought really to be restricted to being read on the spot. It is a big book about Africa, with colour plates showing lions, elephants, rhinoceros and other wild animals. Despite that, Joseph agreed to entrust it to Isidore, urging him to mind what he did. But Isidore totally misunderstood what Joseph meant by this warning, because he immediately put up his hands like a boxer, saying that he wasn't afraid.

I suppose I'm telling you these stories about the Lipsztejns to show you that nothing has really changed here at the Manoir.

By the way, on that subject, if you still have the issue of Droit et Liberté *where they published the photo of us all on the front steps with Marc Chagall, look at it carefully: you can see that Félix is making a V sign at one of the counsellors. When he saw the paper, the counsellor was furious and everyone seemed to take his side against Félix, who was called up to Louba's study. When the two of them came out a short while later, Félix's eyes were red, but Louba announced that all he meant was to give a V for Victory, as he had seen people do in newspaper photographs at the time of the Liberation.*

Otherwise, we are starting to think about holidays. A delegation of children has been invited to spend July in Poland. I don't yet know if I'll be on it and I don't even know if I want to. I think I would prefer to meet up with my friends from last year in summer camp. They are talking about Saint-Jean-de-Luz or Tarnos, on the Basque coast, for this year. Perhaps we'll see each other? I hope so anyway. A lot of children don't want to meet up again this summer in camp after a whole year in the home together, but except for a few who will be going to an uncle or an aunt, most unfortunately have no choice.

They are also saying that at the start of next term the big ones will leave the Manoir and go to another home closer to Paris. The boys will go to Montreuil and the big girls to Arcueil. It's quite sad, leaving these big grounds, which I'm fond of, in spite of everything, but because we will be close to the metro, everything will be easier: Paris, school and lots of things like the cinema, which I do miss a lot.

Write and tell me what you are doing for the holidays. Perhaps between now and then some of you could get together and come to see us one Sunday? Or else we could arrange a trip to Paris, in which case we might all meet up in the Place de la République?

Until one or other of these plans bears fruit, my warmest regards,

Georges

Problems at School

'Do you know Leibelè barks with a Yiddish accent?'

Leibelè is what Isy calls his dog. It's a large dog with long hair over its eyes and it follows Isy around everywhere. He ties it to his handcart when he does the rounds of the apartment blocks, trying to buy old things, such as odd bits of china or unwanted clothes.

He called his dog Leibelè as a tribute to Trotsky.* This enraged Albert, even though he's not a Trotskyite.

'When you respect someone, you don't give his name to an animal,' Albert said, the first time Isy came with his dog.

'Leibelè is not a normal animal,' Isy replied. 'He's a loyal creature – just as Trotsky was loyal to Lenin.'

'There you are! It's impossible to talk politics with you. You confuse everything. As for that dog of yours, I'd call it "dog".'

*Leibelè is an affectionate diminutive of Léon.

'He wouldn't answer to that.'

'So much the better! Since we don't have anything to say to each other anyway, it's just as well.'

And Albert picked up his scissors.

What drove Albert particularly mad was Isy walking around. 'When a man has responsibilities, he struggles to look after his family, or else he's a *schnorrer*.' So Albert stays all day in the shop, and if he goes out, it's only to make a delivery or to bring back work. 'Because there are those who work and those who walk around. That's how it is in this world. And it's not by walking around that you get somewhere in life.'

As far as Albert is concerned, my brother Isy goes around trusting in luck. And when luck happens to favour him, instead of saying, 'It's a good day, luck's on my side, I mustn't stop now,' quite the opposite! Luck, for Isy, is doing a good deal in the morning, which means you can be free the rest of the day. So he immediately goes and puts his cart away in his shed in the Rue des Jardins-Saint-Paul, takes his fishing rod and goes to the river below the Pont Marie to 'tickle some trout', as he says.

'Isy,' I tell him, 'when luck is with you, go on, chase her, stay with her for a while. Why are you satisfied with so little?'

'If I chase after her, Leiélè, I might overtake her

without noticing and then she will be behind me. If you want to catch a fish, you must cast the line at just the right spot and let it float at the same speed as the current – exactly the same speed as the current, without holding it back or pushing it on.'

When his poor wife Hélène is tired of eating fish, Isy brings us some. But as soon as his back is turned, the fish goes straight in the dustbin. I don't even mention it to Albert: who needs any more arguments?

Isy made the remark about Leibelè's Jewish accent to Betty, who was in bed.

She came back from school yesterday afternoon with her teeth chattering and went straight to lie down without eating her tea. The only thing I could get out of her, while she was drinking a glass of hot milk and honey, was that she didn't want to go back to school.

This morning, putting my hand on her forehead, I decided that her temperature had gone down, but I felt she should spend another day in bed.

'I want to change schools,' she also told Isy.

'Change schools?' Isy looked at me. 'But you can't change school just like that, for no reason.'

'It's not for no reason! Anyway, Raphaël changed schools.'

She's right, he did. It was just after the Liberation, shortly after the start of term. Raphaël had a fight with another boy, who called him a dirty Jew. He was so beside himself that the teacher had to get several other boys to help him, because he couldn't restrain Raphaël on his own. Then he slapped Raphaël, because you're not allowed to fight in class. At this, Raphaël went wild with fury and started to shout: 'The war's over! The war's over!' He butted the teacher in the stomach and started to kick the tables. Then he tore up the geography maps that were hanging on the wall and ran out of the school. One of the cleaning women brought Raphaël's satchel back home. Raphaël stayed in bed the next day and he said he didn't want to go back to that school. I was then summoned by the headmaster. He wanted Raphaël to apologize for head-butting the teacher and, most of all, for tearing up the maps of France. So I enrolled Raphaël at the Lycée Charlemagne.

'Did someone call you a dirty Jew at school?' asked Isy, who knew the story about Raphaël.

Betty shook her head.

'But it was something serious, even so?'

Without looking at anybody, Betty nodded.

'And yet it's something you don't want to talk about – not to me, or to your mother, or to anyone?'

Betty shook her head again.

'Something you're ashamed of?'

Betty looked up and her mouth opened, but she didn't speak. Then she quickly lowered her eyes and Isy and I just had time to see that there were tears gathering under her eyelids.

'Listen, here's what we'll do,' Isy said quickly. 'I'll make a deal with you. You tell me your story, and I'll tell you one. OK?'

'You start!'

'I'll start if you like. I think I can trust you.'

In order to hear Isy better, Betty slipped under the bedclothes until only her head was showing.

'Good. Now you listen, too, Leibelè, because it might interest you.'

Leibelè was lying on the ground with his head between his front paws, but he opened an eye when he heard his name. He gave a long yawn, as dogs do, then resumed his former position and went straight back to sleep. For the first time that day, I saw a little smile on Betty's lips.

'That's your tough luck,' Isy said. 'I'll start anyway.

'Once upon a time there was a king whose kingdom was somewhere in central Europe. More precisely, it was in the Carpathians, and, still more precisely than that, it was in the province of Bukovin . . . No, I'll start again. That wasn't a good start. It's very important to find the right opening for a story.'

Isy seemed to be thinking for a moment.

'Here we are: this is the story of a little boy, aged seven, whose name was Jacob. He lived with his parents in a small town in the Austro-Hungarian Empire. When he was very small, Jacob almost died, because when he was born he had something wrong with his respiratory tract. Doctors had tried to treat him, but they had proved unable to overcome the child's illness, which was so serious that his parents had to watch over him day and night. One day Jacob's parents heard tell of a great surgeon, a man called Bronstein, who practised in a clinic in Vienna. His skill and knowledge had saved patients from death, even though other doctors, some of international renown, had given them up for lost.

'This doctor's popularity was so great that you had to make an appointment many weeks, or even many months, in advance for an operation. But, luckily for little Jacob, Bronstein loved children and he was especially keen on desperate cases. Jacob's parents were filled with hope and joy when, in reply to their letter, the clinic wrote giving them an appointment for the following week. However, there was a note at the bottom of the letter which surprised them. It was written in the surgeon's own handwriting and was addressed to Jacob's father: "Since you are a tailor," Dr Bronstein wrote, "bring a bag of buttons along with the boy." And he had signed it.

'They tried in vain to understand what the note meant, but even so the father got together in a little bag, which he made specially, all the buttons he could find: buttons of every colour; metal, wood and bone buttons; trouser buttons, shirt buttons, coat buttons, military buttons, press fasteners . . .

'When they got to Vienna, little Jacob was very weak, because all the hustle and bustle in the city made it extremely hard for him to breathe. In view of the child's state, Dr Bronstein decided to operate that same day.

'The operation lasted four hours and Jacob's parents were sick with worry. When at last they saw the surgeons coming out of the operating theatre covered in sweat but smiling broadly, they fell into each other's arms, weeping for joy, because they realized that the boy was saved. Dr Bronstein explained to them that he had attached a little tube to the trachea, and that this tube ended in a little bone button, carefully chosen from among those that Jacob's father had brought. Thanks to the four small holes by which it's usually sewn on, this little button, grafted on at the larynx, would allow the air to circulate once more through the lungs. "Your little Jacob will now have an almost normal life," Dr Bronstein added. "Or, at least, he will be out of danger. But he ought to leave town as soon as possible." And the doctor advised them to go and live in an area which was considered excellent for the respiratory tract, situated in the Carpathian Mountains – to be precise, in the province of Bukovin.

'Two years went by. Two years during which little

Jacob's parents no longer had to live in anguish. But Jacob, for his part, was not happy. The little bone button that Dr Bronstein had grafted on to him allowed him to breathe normally, but the air passing through it turned the button into a whistle. And since he was now breathing regularly, Jacob's presence was always detectable by a little whistling sound.

'Of course Jacob could come and go without fear, and the sound given out by the little whistle was quite soft and harmonious, but Jacob was unhappy because he was different from other children.

'Jacob felt most out of place at school. Even so, driven by his desire to make up for the time he had lost trying to survive, he had become an excellent student. The teacher often called him up to the board, to serve as an example, but everything that Jacob said in answer to his questions was punctuated by the whistling sound coming from the little bone button. This delighted his classmates, who made fun of him, often very cruelly. So it was that, on his ninth birthday, Jacob decided not to go back to school.

'He spent most of his time in the nearby forest.

'There was a very ancient legend about it in that part of the country: a king had established his kingdom in the very heart of the forest and, so the legend told, this king was able to perform miracles. But, in his great wisdom, the king had made the gates of his kingdom inaccessible, so no one could boast of having got near to it. Yet there were very many people who wanted to see him perform miracles, because the legend was famous well beyond the Carpathians. However, every attempt failed. In reality, the forest was full of invisible beings who protected the king, using slings to hurl little stones with astonishing precision. These stones never hit the people who tried to enter the kingdom, but struck the ground a few centimetres away from them, so that they had to turn back.

'Little Jacob had also heard about the king who could work miracles and had tried several times to enter the forest so that the king could achieve the miracle of miracles and stop the famous little whistling sound which made Jacob the laughing stock of his schoolmates.

'On several occasions he had managed to make his way to places where there was no longer any trace of a path, because he was small and had learned to move with the agility of a cat. But in the end even he was forced to turn back, because each time his little whistle betrayed him, and small stones began to fall around his feet. One day, when he was especially desperate, Jacob was sitting on a large stone at the edge of the forest when suddenly, standing in front of him, he saw an old man. The old man was like one of those you see in picture books, and his face was lit up by a strange light.

Jacob was struck dumb because he could see that it was a supernatural apparition.

'The strange personage asked Jacob why he was in despair.

'"I want to die," Jacob replied.

'"No, Jacob." (The old man knew his name.) "No, Jacob, you do not want to die. You want to live, but you don't know how. You want to meet the king so that he can perform a miracle, but a miracle has to be deserved."

'Jacob did not understand, so the old man explained.

'"Do you know what warns the inhabitants of the forest that you are coming? It's the peculiar whistling that escapes from your throat, which is not like the call of any of the birds living in this forest. This is why, when you approach, the birds stop singing and their silence is what warns of your coming. So here is what we shall do. Every morning we shall meet, the two of us, by this large stone and every morning I shall teach you the song of a bird. In that way, you can continue to breathe, but the air that goes through the little bone button will turn into a melody, and you will be able to sit at ease beside the king and beg him to grant your wish."

'And that is what they did.

'The first morning, Joseph learned the song of the bullfinch with its sweet and melancholy call; the next day, the chattering of the chiff-chaff; the day after that, the lively twitter of the goldfinch; on the fourth day, the linnet's melodious song; and, afterwards, the robin's trilling call and the strident note of the grasshopper warbler. Then, he learned the *tschrl* of the skylark, the *karreu karreu* of the reed warbler and the *youdut youdut* of the song-thrush. Later, the *tak tak* of the blackbird, the *trru trrru* of the blue tit, the ringing call of the chaffinch and the sharp *sib sib sib* of the jenny wren, which only weighs five grammes. Later still, it was the turn of the shrike, with its voice of alarm, the varied babblings of the jay, and the wheatear's chit-chat. He also learned the mocking voice of the starling, the anxious tones of the golden oriole, the *ziwitt ziwitt* of the swallow, the magpie's cackle and the cuckoo's *cuckoo cuckoo*.

'One morning, the day after Jacob had learned the song of the nightingale, the bird that sings even by night with a song as clear as crystal, he went as usual to the large rock. But that day the wise man didn't come. At this, Jacob understood that his training was over. Without a moment's hesitation, he set off.

'Awake to the slightest sound, he felt he could understand the language of the birds and recalled what the sage had told him on the first morning: "You have only to listen to understand what they are singing." And what he imagined would be a daunting trial turned into something like a game, because he knew the birds' songs off by heart.

'Suddenly, when he had almost forgotten why he was in the forest, Jacob came out into a vast clearing. It was radiant with light, the same light that had surrounded the face of the old man who had taught Jacob so much. In the midst of the clearing, with his back to the forest, was a man sitting on a throne.

'Jacob remained rooted to the spot, unable to utter a word.

'"Come and sit beside me," said the king, without turning round.

'Awestruck, Jacob obeyed the king and went to sit beside him. Only then did he see, to his astonishment, that it was the sage of the large rock. At first he wondered why the king had demanded so many weeks of effort from him, when – since he had the power to do so – he could very well have performed the little miracle the first time they met, which would have allowed Jacob to become a little boy like the others.

'However, he dutifully answered the king's questions.

'The king listened attentively to Jacob and replied that he could do nothing further for him. At this, Jacob's heart was heavy with grief.

'"So, did I come here for nothing?" he said, letting the tears run down his cheeks.

'The king took the child's hands in his own, which were large and white, and spoke kindly to him.

'"No, my little Jacob, you didn't come here for nothing. You must realize why it was that you succeeded in overcoming all the obstacles. If you came to see me in the hope of becoming a child like all the rest, then you were wrong, because you will never be a child who is quite like any other. However, you must know that, in coming this far, you have achieved something extraordinary, because there are very few in each generation who manage to follow this road. The miracle cannot come from me, because it consists in the very fact of having reached this place. That is the miracle that I hoped for from you, and that is why you did the right thing by coming."'

Here, Isy stopped.

'Is that all?' asked Betty.

'That's all,' Isy said.

Betty thought for a while.

'I didn't really understand the ending.'

'One doesn't always understand a story right away, but that's not important. What matters is to listen, and to retell the story when you know it. Do you remember the deal we made? I tell you a story and you tell yours. But, don't forget, you must find the right beginning for a story. I've talked a lot, so I'll go and drink a glass of water. I'll be back soon.'

Leibelè opened his eye again when Isy got up to go out, but he must have realized that his master was going to return because he went back to sleep again.

To encourage Betty, I raised her pillow, thinking that she would be better able to tell the story sitting up.

Isy came back and sat down again on his chair without saying anything.

'It was because of the essay,' Betty said after a short pause.

'The essay?'

'I wrote *humersot*.'

'So?'

'So the mistress told me that you don't say *humersot*, you say somersault. But before that, she asked me what it meant. And as I couldn't explain properly, I stood up in front of her desk and did one and then the elastic on my knickers snapped and everyone made fun of me.'

Because children are like that, Betty began to cry bitterly. One could sense that the tears were coming because she spoke faster and faster, as you do when you are afraid you might not be able to finish what you are saying. I took her in my arms and hugged her, and tried to console her by saying that it wasn't serious, but she was inconsolable, with a real little girl's sorrow.

Isy was also wondering how to stop Betty's tears;

suddenly, seeing Leibelè, who was wide awake because of the crying, he said:

'You don't know what a *humersot* is, either, do you Leibelè? Well, you're as silly as the schoolmistress. What? All right, watch carefully and I'll show you.'

And, with a little run-up, Isy did a somersault. But, as he went past, he caught a chair with his foot and it nearly fell on his head. Leibelè thought this was some new game and began to run round Isy, barking so loudly that Albert rushed out of the workshop.

'What is it? What's going on? What's wrong with you?' he asked Isy, seeing him on the floor.

'I did a *humersot*,' Isy replied, holding his knee, which he had hurt. 'Didn't I, Leibelè?'

Leibelè went *woof! woof!*

'See, Albert, my people's commissar said, "*Yup, yup.*"'

The next day Betty went back to school.

The Extent of Happiness

When you are trying to calm someone down or to ease their pain, you listen while they talk. Sometimes you want to take their hand. Sometimes, you even want to put your arms round them, but there are people with whom you can't do this, because just listening to them is an encouragement. And then they go too far, because you've encouraged them.

Léa went too far.

As he often does on Fridays, Albert has gone to fetch some supplies from Wasserman's and, since it's the start of the slack season, Mme Andrée and the other finishers haven't come in today, nor has Léon. Maurice left at around four o'clock. Léa is sitting in Mme Andrée's place. She has brought me a glass of tea. After drinking it, I put the glass down on the little table used by the finishers. Now Léa is holding it between her hands as if to warm them.

Today she has not just been keeping me company. There were things she wanted to tell me. I got the feeling that all was not well between her and Albert.

Also, there was a certain intimacy in the conversation and I rather let myself go.

This is not the first time Léa has been here, sitting in Mme Andrée's place and talking to me after making me tea, but it's the first time she has talked like this, about us. About herself and me. Particularly about herself. Léa's arms are round and I think she is beautiful. She has large dark eyes.

'When you talk to me, you always say such nice things. It makes me feel so good.'

'It makes me feel good, too, Léa. That's why I was wrong to say them to you.'

'No, Charles, you weren't wrong. There is wisdom in you and your calm manner also does me good.'

'Don't be fooled by the conversations we have like this; I've also got a dreadful temper.'

'Temper? Yes, that's true ... But even so, it's only when I'm with you that I feel good.'

'Listen, Léa, I'm very happy here in the shop and I don't want to have to leave. And do you know why I'm very happy here? Because Albert does everything to make me happy. When there is no work left for the others, there's always some for me. And when he goes to make a delivery, I know quite well that he asks you to keep me company a little so that I won't feel so lonely, because he has such trust in you and such trust in me. In fact that's why we started to talk to one another. Albert wants to please me and help me along, but he can't tell me so. I don't know how to explain . . .'

'But he doesn't talk to me either, he doesn't tell me things that make me feel good – and I'm his wife. Is it so difficult to tell your wife that you love her? I need to hear someone say that they love me.'

'And that's the sort of thing people say, is it?'

'Some people do.'

'And would that satisfy you?'

'It's nice to hear it.'

'It must be nice to hear it, since you say so. But, Léa, you have to understand, it's not that there are two Alberts: there's only one. That's how Albert is. You know, I think it's precisely because he does things that he can't say them. You remember when little Joseph came in as a presser to replace Léon, last season? Every evening Albert spent about an hour at the press putting Joseph's work right. And Joseph never knew a thing about it. No one told him: not Albert, not the rest of the shop. And that was more important than telling him that he was very fond of him, even though you may not think so.'

There was a silence after that, as there had been a few times since Léa came to bring me the glass of tea. We both knew that, during these pauses, the conversation between Léa and myself continued in our heads. This is why we didn't always pick it up where we had left off. For Léa to come in like that, to sit down for a moment and chat – that we could always do and it's true that it did me good. But not if there was something going on at the back of my mind: those ideas ought to be left where they are. Unfortunately, they are not always ready to go away of their own accord.

As I was trying to go on with my sewing at the machine, it was Léa who resumed our conversation.

'I can't go through my whole life not knowing whether I'm loved. And it's not me Albert loves, it's the family.'

'That's the same thing.'

'No. It's not the same thing any more.'

'It's not the same thing any more and it's still the same thing. Before there were the children, there was only you. I don't know if Albert used to say he loved you, but he didn't need to tell you so, to love you, and you didn't ask, and that was fine. But since Betty and Raphaël arrived and he has loved them as well as you, you've panicked. You insist that he should prove his love for you with words. You say that what he loves is his family? Yes, he does. It is his family that he loves. But if you were to go out of his life, what would be left of his family? Albert would have nothing except a family that was sick and crippled.'

'Are you trying to persuade me that Albert is a good head of the family? Yes, he's a good head of the family. And a good father, too. I've never denied it. Albert does everything he has to do, that's true, but no more. And that more is precisely what I need. Charles, I want you to understand that I can't stand it any longer, being the wife who looks after her husband and children. I can't stand being nothing to my husband except the sensible wife who does her wifely duty.'

'And for your part?'

'How do you mean, for my part?'

'Your feelings for Albert?'

'I told you: I'm not happy and I need to be happy to love. Even so, I think I have been happy with Albert. Sometimes before we were married, he would kiss me in the street, and I didn't want him to, because I was ashamed of being seen. And he used to give me presents. Little presents, of course, because we didn't have much money. One day, without telling me, he wrote to his mother in Poland telling her to buy me a large black shawl with big coloured flowers on it, like you only find over there. That shawl was almost the last news we got from Poland, just before war broke out. At the Liberation, I gave it to the lady who had hidden Betty and me in the country . . . I think I regret it a little now . . . Yes, it was definitely a mistake because that was the present that pleased me most of all. Nowadays, Albert doesn't buy me presents any more. He tells me to buy what I want. "Since the work is going well," he tells me, "go on, buy what you want."'

'And do you buy what you want?'

'Sometimes. But I don't even know if he notices.'

As I realized that Léa knew that I realized what she was trying to say, I knew that the discussion had to end. But I didn't know how to end it. I was afraid of being clumsy and, like an idiot, I went on sewing without saying a word.

'During the war,' Léa continued, 'it wouldn't have occurred to me to wonder if we were any less in love. I missed Albert and there was no room for anything except anxiety. Now Albert is here, yet I feel that he is going away from me; or perhaps I am the one who is going away from him. It's as if I no longer exist. I feel very alone. Of course, you really are alone, but I feel alone even with my husband . . . I'm afraid of suddenly getting old and no longer wanting to struggle to be happy. It's when I think, "Give up happiness", that I am most afraid, because that is the end of everything. And perhaps that fear is what drives me to commit what you think is madness.'

Everything was confused in my head, because Léa had said what she wanted to tell me. I don't know how she managed to say it, but she repeated that she felt good with me. So good that she knew I would make her happy, and other things apart from that which I didn't take in because I decided that it was absolutely essential to wipe my spectacles, so blurred was my vision. And all these questions occurred to me at the same time. Is Léa really the unhappy wife that she claims to be? What does it mean, to have a husband, and children, and be unhappy? It doesn't make any sense! And what is the life that she wants to have with me? And why me? Has she taken pity on me to such an extent that she is ready to break up her home? That doesn't make any sense, either. To make a new life for oneself: what does it mean, to make a new life? Make a new life, when a life is still in the process of being made? Does Léa need anyone else to make a new life?

'What is it Léa? Are you feeling sorry for me, or what? You know that I shall say no, because of Albert, so you think that it will console me to know that a young woman is ready to give up everything, to sacrifice her family and make a new life with me. Is that it? Are you proud of that idea? It's not a good thing that you are doing, Léa, not good.'

'Do I look like someone who feels sorry? It's true that you've suffered a lot, and no doubt that explains your temper and those silences of yours that hurt me so much . . .'

'Stop looking for excuses all the time for the ones who have suffered! We don't have a right to behave as

we like, because we have suffered. And other people –
what rights do they have? Doesn't Albert have a right
to happiness?'

'I'm talking about myself, Charles, about what I feel.
On Sundays when I go through the empty workshop,
I always look at your machine and my heart starts to
beat faster. That's how I came to realize that I need
you . . . In the evening, when the children have gone
to bed, often Albert and I don't exchange a single word.
At such times I think of you. What Albert is thinking
about, I don't know, but perhaps he's thinking of someone else as well, I don't know.'

'I suppose you hope so?'

'No, no. I'm not saying that. It's stupid, but I'm still
jealous. Sometimes, in the evening, when I'm doing the
washing up . . . It embarrasses me to say it . . .'

I did nothing to encourage Léa to carry on, though
I was glad that she was talking about Albert again. And
since there are some things which are easier to say when
you don't have to look someone in the eye, I got up to
check the hang of a sleeve on a dummy. The silence
must have been still more awkward for Léa, so she went
on:

'Sometimes, when I'm doing the dishes, Albert comes
up behind me and kisses me. I talk to him about the
children, who are not yet asleep, because I don't even
know if it's me he's thinking about at that moment.'

'It's you he's thinking about, Léa, you and no one else.'

'What makes you so sure?'

'Because I'm sure.'

I went and sat down again, but left the sleeve on the dummy – with what I had to tell Léa, I couldn't carry on working.

'Listen, Léa. In any event, you are wrong about me. Because I'm here every day and because you think I'm available, you have transformed me into someone else. I'm not quite certain what kind of man you are dreaming about. Perhaps he doesn't exist, and if he does, it's more likely to be the man who has left to get the supplies from Wasserman's. It can't be me. What has got into you, Léa? Do you want to deprive Betty and Raphaël of their father? And Albert of his children? Look at Albert's eyes when he sees his children coming back from school. Look at them carefully. You have to learn to recognize happiness when you have it. And learn to keep it, even if you have to fight for it, before other people set about destroying it. How can you imagine that I could deprive Albert of his children? I could never again look him in the face, nor his children, nor anyone else. It would drive me mad for the rest of my life. Now, if you want to carry on talking, talk. I can't stop you. But stop thinking about me. Don't worry about my loneliness, or my happiness, or my life. You are not "Hello-hello", whose mission in life is to bring happiness to those who are unattached. You are Léa, you have a husband and two children, and I am not free. I am occupied. I'm occupied by my memories . . . You dream of a nice house, of being entertained and of having a wonderful husband who will tell you all day long that he loves you; and you imagine that I could say these tender words to you . . . Listen to me, now, Léa. I am sure that this conversation is not good, because it has led you too far, but since we have started, there are things that I must tell you: you feel lonely and you want a miracle to happen. Well, don't expect the miracle from me. I'm not a miracle-worker. I didn't leave my wife and she didn't leave me. We were separated, that's all. I'm not alone. We lived together for ten years. I have memories to last me a lifetime. They are enough for me. Some happiness is brief and some is long. Mine lasted ten years. There you are, ten years: that is the extent of my happiness. Happiness, real happiness, in my view, is to have the chance and the opportunity to have a calm life. When I think of the ten years that I spent with my wife, the image that sums up our happiness is that of the long periods of calm that we shared. My past is enough to keep me company and that's what fills my life. Don't dream of being my wife, Léa. I'm not a man for the future. I live in the present because it allows me to remember – and if I don't remember, who will? You mustn't try to take Ella's place. You mustn't try, because she is no longer here to defend it. She only has me left to protect her.'

Léa seemed very small, sitting on Mme Andrée's chair. Naturally, she was crying and so was I.

'I just wanted to tell you, Léa, that I need calm. Just calm. That's what my life is made up of now – of calm. And don't think that I'm indifferent to your presence in the shop when we are alone. It sweetens my afternoons and the glass of tea you bring me warms my heart more than you can know. But all this conversation is pointless because it is leading nowhere, and because it's leading nowhere, it must stop.'

'Do you imagine it was easy to say what I said? Do you imagine I haven't been thinking about it for weeks and weeks? I've never heard of a divorce in my family and I honestly can't think of a divorce among the people I know. I know that divorce is a catastrophe. So you must believe me when I tell you that I feel very unhappy. Perhaps I've dreamed too much, or perhaps I got married too young. I don't know. But I'd like to know what you should do when your belly aches because a particular man is looking at you and your heart beats so hard that you think it will stop beating altogether. That, too, was difficult to say, but if I hadn't said it now, I should never have had the courage to say it.'

'You're mad, Léa . . . Or perhaps not. But you are mad to say that to me. It's better that I should leave straight away. But before I do so, I want to tell you another story. It was when Albert was still in Poland and he was seventeen years old. He was very good friends with a boy of his own age, and this boy, for some reason which no one knows, couldn't stand his younger brother, who was thirteen, I think. Albert was upset when he saw the things that the older boy inflicted on the younger one, and one day, for no reason, he slapped the little boy as hard as he could. Yes, the little one. At first the older brother was astonished, and then, absolutely disgusted at what he saw as a terribly unfair act, he in turn violently slapped Albert, who did not protest. They never spoke again. Many years afterwards they were all living in Paris. It was just before war broke out. The two brothers were business partners: they had become inseparable. And, a few years after that, the brothers were arrested on the same day and deported in the same train.'

'Albert has never told me that story.'

'When he told it to me, he was weeping. And, you know, I think that I understand the story better now that I, in turn, have told it to you. It is as though, in telling it aloud, I understood something that I didn't know before. Well, there you are. Now I think I should leave. If Albert asks why I haven't finished the work,

tell him . . . I don't know, tell him whatever you want
. . . Goodnight, Léa.'

Léa wished me goodnight too. As I was going down
the stairs, I imagined her alone in the room, sitting for
a moment at Mme Andrée's place before making up
her mind to take the empty glass back to the kitchen,
with, as usual, a small amount of strawberry jam at the
bottom which had not been stirred in.

'Paula, Paula'

'Why do you need a tape measure now? Do you want to find out whether a dash of the iron can turn a size 42 into a size 46?'

I had borrowed the tape measure which M. Albert always carries around his neck simply to measure a parcel wrapped in a magazine and held together by string, which Mme Paulette had put down beside her when she came in.

'Twenty centimetres by twenty! Precisely the size of a packet of matzos. If you are ashamed to walk down the street with a packet of matzos from Rosinski's, Madame Paulette, go and buy a baguette, it will attract less attention.'

'You think you're clever, don't you?'

As for saying that I thought I was especially clever, you couldn't. And in fact I didn't say so. I didn't because Mme Paulette got on my nerves. Not that she got on my nerves like the assimilated Jews – who, in fact, stopped getting on my nerves as soon as I realized that they didn't really feel Jewish. Moreover, ever since they came in for their fair share of surprises – what with the yellow star, Drancy and the road towards that East Europe, which they so despised – they have felt more like brothers to me; or rather, I have felt more like a brother to them, since the ones who came back from it all will definitely remain Jews until the end of their days.

But Mme Paulette was not assimilated. Her matzos (even wrapped in a magazine), her accent, her presence in the workshop, were all obstacles in the way of assimilation. More simply, Mme Paulette got on my nerves because I had the impression that the Jewess she was, was ashamed of being one.

However, I felt neither pleased nor displeased with myself as I went to give M. Albert back his tape measure before returning to my pressing table.

M. Albert always kept his tape measure around his neck, a habit he had got into in the days when everything was 'made to measure'. As he mentions from time to time, M. Albert was someone in tailoring. During the war, when he worked for M. Dumaillet, the tailor in the Rue de Sèvres who had hidden him in an attic room, M. Albert had plenty of free time, all alone, and had spent it inventing a method of cutting that could be summarized in two pages and which, normally, might have qualified him to stand beside the inventors of cutting methods, like Napolitano, if he had thought to have it published. But as M. Albert said, 'Mine was only an emergency method, since it could be folded in four and put in a waistcoat pocket.' And he added that it should only be used in the event of all other methods disappearing. M. Albert's method was based on the following principle: for a garment to hang properly, it must be put together so that all the seams or darts pass through certain points on the body, such as the centre of the chest, the nape of the neck, the line of the shoulders, the waistline, the depth of the arm-hole, the top of the elbow, etc. M. Albert had drawn up figures and a sketch on a single page showing the position and distances between these points for a size 44 and, on another page, more figures and another diagram to give a sliding scale for other sizes. From it, you could make up any model you wanted.

Even though, unfortunately, most tailors were wiped out in the war, there were, *Gott tzu dank*,* a few survivors who could remember the traditional cutting techniques, so M. Albert folded the sheet of paper with his method and stored it in a drawer.

However, fine tailor though he is, because of his

*'Thank God!'

gratitude towards M. Dumaillet, the last suit Albert made for himself is unlined at the back.

M. Dumaillet sometimes comes to the workshop to say hello to M. Albert and Mme Léa. When he arrived with the news that his son was getting married, M. Albert volunteered to make a suit for both father and son as a wedding present. But since the Dumaillets had asked no one's advice before fixing the date of the wedding, it fell, needless to say, right in the middle of the busy season. As a result, because of the two fittings and despite nights spent in the shop finishing the two promised garments (between ourselves, the father's three-piece suit was perfect), M. Albert did not have time to finish off the one he was making for himself.

'Just imagine!' Mme Léa said, slightly ashamed. 'A tailor wearing a jacket with no lining!'

'Who's going to look inside?' M. Albert replied; and he went through the whole ceremony without unbuttoning his jacket.

On the subject of Dumaillet, I always called him Du Mayer, so Jacqueline was absolutely convinced that M. Dumaillet was a Jew and that Dumaillet was just a name that he had picked for himself during the war and kept afterwards.

'But Jacqueline,' I told her, 'if he had been a Jew, he would not have been called *du* Mayer, but just Mayer.'

'People say Baron *de* Rothschild.'

'That's true, you're quite right, except that M. Dumaillet is not a baron.'

'Then why do you always call him Du Mayer, if he's not a Jew or a baron?'

I don't remember exactly what I replied to that. The truth is that I thought, because of the risks he took to help M. Albert during the war, he deserved to be called that; but of course I couldn't say so.

M. Albert is not satisfied with just making bespoke suits for M. Dumaillet and his son. From time to time, taking his tape measure and chalk, and with a pincushion attached to his forearm, he goes into a little room before you get to the workshop where the lengths of cloth are stored, which is usually reserved for 'bespoke' customers. As if to apologize for accepting the additional work, he says that it's to keep his hand in. In my opinion, it's chiefly to fill in time during the slack season and not to have to stay and watch us making the few garments that have to be delivered to Wasserman's.

At times, made-to-measure work can bring surprises. One day, M. Albert came back from the little room with his arms wide apart.

'Do you know what this is, Léon? It's the bust size of the lady who has just gone out.'

'You measured her with your arms?'

'*H'ouh'em!** It's the most astonishing bust I've ever seen. An American lady. Approximately 160 centimetres.'

'Approximately? Are you using approximations nowadays, Monsieur Albert? Where did you leave your tape measure?'

'My tape measure? Too short. When I saw that it wouldn't go round, I didn't dare make a mark so that I could measure the bit that was left. I assessed it by eye. Has any of you ever seen a bust like that?'

As he asked the question, M. Albert glanced mechanically at Maurice and I think he must have regretted it, because, without waiting for a reply, he turned back to his cutting table, perhaps thinking that in the past few years the people Abramauschwitz had met might have fitted several to the one tape measure.

To return to Mme Paulette and her magazines, she doesn't only use them to wrap around packets of matzos. She reads them, too, and then she talks about fashionable people as though she knew them. She even refers to them occasionally by their first names. Sometimes, making fun, I talk like her: 'Oh, look, *Edith*'s going to be on at the ABC.' But Mme Paulette doesn't realize. She says, 'Yes, I know,' then tells you about Edith Piaf's

*Clever dick.

probable next husband. Because that's what mainly interests her: marriage and divorce.

After all this time, I shouldn't care about Mme Paulette's boasting, but it does irritate me. With her, it's always: 'Yes, I've already seen it, I've already read it.' Her favourite phrase is always: 'I know that.' Sometimes she adds (especially when talking to me), '. . . better than you do'. At this, I can't stop myself from getting into an argument with her, trying to catch her out.

Once, to set a trap for her, I made up a name, pretending he was some new actor, and invented a whole story to go with it. And when, once again, she told me that she knew all about it, I expected to score a point when I revealed the trick. But what did Mme Paulette answer? 'I know that, I said it on purpose.'

There is no place in Mme Paulette's mind for the possibility that I might ever be right. Especially not more often than her. But she has an excuse: she doesn't really know what being right is. She can't understand that being right means saying things in accordance with what you know or with common sense. She thinks that in life people ought to be right in turns, like when we used to queue at the baker's, and added to that there should be a system of priority – old people are necessarily more often right than young ones. And she always ends with the same argument: 'Why do you always have to be right?'

She puts it down to my character.

I have to admit that all these arguments are of no great interest to me; how could they be, since even when I do catch her out, she gives a forced laugh that sounds like 'hi-hi-hi!', against which I am powerless, because there is no answer to a forced laugh. To me, a laugh is 'ha-ha-ha!'. But not for Mme Paulette. For her, it's 'hi-hi-hi!'. At times like these she annoys me so much that I save ten minutes on the ironing of a garment and I am the one to stop the argument, because you can't save ten minutes on every piece without it having an effect on the quality of the work.

Kinman, the director of the Yiddish Theatre, once told me that with a theatre company the day he concentrates most is when he is handing out the parts. And that you shouldn't give an actor a role where he is playing himself; you should give him a taste for being someone else and an opportunity to play it.

In his editions of the plays which he directed, he noted down remarks by Louis Jouvet. He had had long conversations with Jouvet. I remembered some of the remarks:

'One acts because one has the impression of never having been oneself and at last having the possibility to be so.'

And again:

'An actor wants to escape from himself, to leave himself in order to free himself, find himself, reveal himself; and he wants to escape from mediocrity, convention and the unbearable falsehood of his life.'

'If you ever happen to put on a play,' Kinman also told me, 'give an actor a role which he is not expecting, don't imprison him in a job; he will then be forced to invent, to observe, to imagine, and he will be surprised – if he's a good actor – to see that people are not all of one piece.'

I thought of that after a discussion I had with M. Albert, one day when I arrived early at work and I saw Mme Paulette blowing her nose very hard. It seemed to me that she was using it as a pretext to wipe away a few tears. As that was the first time I'd seen it, I asked M. Albert at an appropriate moment – because, if there was one thing I couldn't imagine, it was Mme Paulette in tears.

'Tears are the only stock that never runs out,' M. Albert said, and he told me Mme Paulette's story.

'I have known Mme Paulette since before the war. We worked in the same shop and in those days they didn't have the same system of payment as we have today. The boss paid the machinist piecework, as now, but for a complete garment, felled and lined, and each machinist had his own finisher, and gave her part of his salary. Naturally, if the finisher couldn't keep up, the machinist fell behind with his work. Mme Paulette was both the finisher and the wife of her machinist, who was so anxious that Mme Paulette wouldn't keep up with him that he was constantly saying, "Paula, Paula", without looking up from his machine. Paula was her real first name. I honestly believe that no one in the shop ever heard him say anything apart from "Paula, Paula". When he had to go to the toilet, the whole workshop would take over and chant in chorus, "Paula, Paula". One day they had enough money to set up on their own. But they didn't open a tailor's. They took a shop in the Rue de Passy or the Rue de la Pompe ... I'm not sure which any longer, but in any case it was somewhere around there, and on the shop-front they wrote: 'Ironing by the minute'. From then on, Paula became Mme Paulette, which was her idea. It's an area where there's a good sort of clientele, and to begin with it worked quite well. There were even actors living around there who often needed a last-minute touch of the iron on an evening dress. People like Pierre Richard Wilm or Georges Grey, she told me, I think, who sometimes took the trouble to drop by in person.

'So Mme Paulette, who sat behind the cash desk and welcomed the customers, suddenly found that she had, in front of her, in the flesh, in her own shop, people whose photos appeared in magazines. At that, she got a touch of *folie de grandeur* and began to imagine that

147

if well-known, important people were talking to her directly, this meant that she was really Mme Paulette, and that she would come to be like these important figures – she believed that she herself was becoming someone important.

'However, the husband, at the back of the shop, well, he'd come to feel like a man who's left his *shtetl* behind for the second time. So, to cheer himself up, he would occasionally come back to see us at the workshop. But for us, the system of work hadn't changed: every machinist with his finisher was trying to get out as many items as possible every day, which meant, of course, that we didn't have much time to talk to him. So he took to frequenting a café just behind the Carreau du Temple where some Jews used to play cards all day long. Here, where they would talk – in Yiddish, too – about the international situation which was just starting to get really bad, Mme Paulette's husband felt at home again. The trouble was that back in the Rue de la Pompe, it wasn't 'ironing by the minute' they should have written, but 'ironing by the day', or even longer. And, despite the evenings spent trying to make up for lost time, the stars became rarer. It was this, above all, that made Mme Paulette really unhappy, not the ruin of the business.'

'And the husband? What happened to him? Was he deported?'

'No, no. As things were starting to go wrong between them, he decided to set off on his own and he took the boat for Argentina. He said that he would write to try to get her to follow him over there.'

'I don't suppose he ever did.'

'I don't suppose so, either. But who knows? In any case, war broke out. Meanwhile, Mme Paulette had sold the shop and became a finisher again.'

'So she stopped mixing with the stars.'

'That's right. But she really did know them, even if not quite in the way she says.'

'In that case, wouldn't it be simpler to explain? She always talks about it as if she is showing off.'

'It's true, sometimes she does show off. Because, as I told you, that was perhaps the only time in her life when she felt truly important. And then, she has to do it, because otherwise she would have to tell the whole story: "Paula, Paula", the cards, Argentina, and the rest. The fact is, I believe Mme Paulette doesn't know any longer whom she really met in her shop. And as she is always reading magazines, she convinces herself that she still knows these famous people.'

After that, and also because of the tears which she had been wiping away with her handkerchief, I decided to let Mme Paulette live in peace with her dreams; and then, one day, after I can't remember what discussion,

she told me that, as I spent all my time criticizing, I
should have been a criticizer in a newspaper.

'Critic, Madame Paulette, not criticizer. Critic. But
you know, Madame Paulette,' I said patiently, 'criticism
can be good as well as bad. Sometimes you hear people
saying, "He made a favourable criticism of the play and
the sets," and things like that. And, quite apart from
that, where do you expect me to find the time to be a
critic? I'm already a presser *and* an actor.'

'Hi, hi, hi.'

That's it! She is starting her *hi-hi-hi* again.

'When a Jew Takes a Blow, He Also Makes an Enemy'*

If you have never had to sew fake fur on the machine, you can congratulate yourself on a lucky escape.

Fake fur is quite different from real fur. You only need to see the fluff flying around the room when it is being sewn on the machine to realize that furriers have no need to worry about the competition.

'What sort of cloth is this?' Jacqueline asked, the day when we were making up the first garment. 'It's going up my nose by the shovelful.'

'Oh, so it's a cloth is it?' said Léon.

His voice cracked as he pronounced the word 'cloth'.

'Fake fur is in fashion this winter,' was all M. Albert said.

It was a good answer, because you can't contradict fashion. And, as the slack season always comes on time,

*Yiddish proverb.

we had no alternative but to spend the winter among clouds of fluff.

'Why is it called "teddy-bear" in French?' Jacqueline asked.

'Because of Theodore Roosevelt,' Charles answered.

Jacqueline sat up and paid attention.

'The American president?'

'Yes, the other one, his cousin.'

'Did he invent this fabric?' Jacqueline went on.

Even Charles smiled at that. What was good about Jacqueline was that you could laugh at what she said, without her ever getting the impression you were making fun of her. And since in any case no one in the room could see any connection with Roosevelt, there was no reason for us to make fun of her.

'No, he didn't invent teddy-bear fabric,' Charles said. 'But Teddy is a diminutive of Theodore, and since he was a great bear hunter, they called him Teddy Bear in English.'

Everyone always admired Charles's general knowledge. You could tell that mainly by the looks and the silences that followed. And in the silence that followed this remark Mme Paulette said, 'Yes, that's right. I knew that.'

Léon had to put his iron down before answering.

You see, Léon's dream was that Mme Paulette should at least once acknowledge her ignorance in front of the whole shop. But he must have asked himself how he could actually prove that she didn't know what she claimed she did; so, to avoid getting into a pointless argument, he thought it best to carry on ironing. Only it was too late, because we could see very well from Léon's expression that whatever pleasure Charles had given him had been spoiled by Mme Paulette's remark.

What I'm coming to is that, because of the fake fur, these days Charles and I would be there, every morning, already at our machines before the others were in their places in the workshop.

I mentioned earlier that Charles rarely took part in discussions. But in the morning, when we are on our own, sitting opposite one another, we do sometimes talk a little.

A few days ago, when I got to work, Léon was also there already. While waiting for his iron to heat up, he had got into a debate with Charles over an article in *Franc-Tireur*, which Léon buys every morning and leaves open on his ironing table.

Three collaborators, who had been journalists on *Je suis partout*, had just been sentenced.* Their trial had lasted a week and a writer in *Franc-Tireur* considered it

---

*The three were Lucien Rebatet, Pierre-Antoine Cousteau and Claude Jeantet. On 23 November 1946 the first two were sentenced to death and the third to hard labour for life.

unjust that two of them had been condemned to death because of what they had written, while some high-ranking officers had only received light sentences. I gathered that Léon agreed with the article, but not Charles.

'There are some pen-holders,' Charles said, 'that are more guilty than rifles. If a soldier or a militiaman arrested and killed Jews and members of the Resistance, it's true that he's guilty and must be sentenced, because once in prison he is no longer a threat. But the journalists on *Je suis partout* are more guilty because they are more dangerous. It was because of their articles that people joined the militia. It was because they wrote "Death to the Jews" that thousands of Jews were arrested by the police. Do you know many people who protested? Do you think that as many Jews would have been denounced if the French hadn't read the things they did in their newspapers? Personally, I felt no pity when Brasillach was shot, and nor will I feel any when it's Rebatet's turn to be executed at the Fort de Montrouge. I won't feel pity because their ideas are like poison. And, unfortunately, the poison will go on circulating, even after their deaths.'*

'I never said I felt sorry for them,' Léon answered,

*Rebatet was not executed. He was pardoned on 12 April 1947, and freed in 1952.

checking the heat of his iron. 'I just said that they didn't have blood on their hands.'

'Yes, they do. They do have blood on their hands. They do, because they are responsible. An intellectual is a responsible person, perhaps the most responsible . . .'

We heard the radio go on in Mme Léa's kitchen. The discussion ended at this point because the finishers would soon be arriving and we hadn't yet taken a single item off the machine. In any event, in the shop an interrupted discussion is always resumed sooner or later. Especially with Léon. He was offered the opportunity to resume this one the very same day when we went for a coffee, he and I, on the corner of the Rue Saint-Claude. As he was stirring his sugar in his cup, he happened to glance towards the counter and suddenly went quite pale.

'Are you all right?'

'I was in prison with that guy,' Léon said, not taking his eyes off the counter.

'In prison?'

I followed his eyes: a man, who didn't look much like a Jew, was leaning against the counter and finishing his coffee.

'Yes. Not for long. One day. But it was enough. He's one I won't ever forget: he's a Fascist.'

The man left without noticing us. When I looked at Léon, he was trying to drink his coffee, but his hand was trembling too much. So he put the cup down and told me about it.

'It was shortly before you joined the workshop. In 1945, April 1945. It began at number 3, Rue des Guillemites, behind the Rue des Francs-Bourgeois. There was this guy who, despite an expulsion order, was refusing to give his home back to a Jew who had just returned from deportation. Once already a bailiff with a police officer had been forced to retreat by a gang that the tenant had got together. This time, too, even though there was a police van outside in the street, some thirty Fascists prevented the eviction and, with some guys rounded up here and there, they immediately organized an anti-Semitic demonstration. There were perhaps five hundred of them in the Rue Vieille-du-Temple, yelling, "France for the French! Death to the Jews!" They were commanded by a lieutenant, in uniform, and they attacked Jews whenever they recognized one.'

'I didn't know the French were like the Poles – that they know how to recognize a Jew.'

'They'd had time to learn. Those ones, at any rate.'

'But I don't get it: surely the militiamen were arrested at the time of the Liberation?'

'Not all of them,' Léon snapped. 'That's why I didn't agree with Charles this morning. There's nothing the Fascists aren't capable of. France had been freed, they were already fighting in the streets of Berlin, and there, in the heart of Paris, Fascists were once more shouting "Death to the Jews!". Since many of them were free, as far as they were concerned, nothing had really changed. You mustn't forget that at that time the trial of Pétain and Laval had not yet taken place. It was only last month at the Nuremberg trials that the Nazi war criminals were sentenced, and then not all of them.'

'But that means Charles is right, about ideas circulating . . .'

'It means we're both right. The guilty must be punished. Not necessarily those who shouted "Death to the Jews!", because if you had to arrest all of those . . . And not for revenge, either, even though it feels good. But because if the guilty are free, then those who died, what did they die for? For nothing?'

'But didn't the police do anything that day?'

'Yes, afterwards. First of all, everyone in the area was informed of what was going on. We caught up with the demonstrators at the Rue du Roi-de-Sicile and there was a real pitched battle. Those who used to say that the Jews were too cowardly to fight must have rued the day they thought as much. When I got there, I found two bastards kicking an old Jew who had fallen on the ground. I thought I'd go mad. I'd seen the first pictures from the camps – I don't have to tell you – and for me what I could see going on in front of my eyes was the same. I've often thought that if I'd had the revolver I was given in the Resistance, I might have killed them. I was still hitting them when the cops arrived.'

'But why did they arrest you?'

'Why? Habit, I suppose. And then they didn't look, they just bundled everyone up together. And the funniest thing, Maurice, is that more Jews were arrested than Fascists. The guy who's just left was one of the Fascists who did end up in the police station with me.'

I felt a shudder run through me and put my hands in my pockets as I do whenever I feel that particular chill. You think you've seen everything and then, having ended up in this free and almost peaceable world, you find Fascism still exists and does not even take the trouble to disguise itself. At the same time, I realized that my presence in the café was a mistake and that I should definitely never have gone there. I didn't even see Jacqueline, who had come down from the shop and was standing in front of me, talking. I didn't understand anything that she was saying or what she wanted. It was only after a bit that I understood that she had come to find us because, she said, Léon and I might have decided to stay in the café chatting, but upstairs she and Mme Andrée and Mme Paulette would soon all be twiddling their thumbs, and if she was to twiddle her thumbs, she might as well do it at home as in the workshop.

The teddy-bear fur was really flying that afternoon in M. Albert's shop.

I haven't told the whole of that story, because you could say that it had certain consequences.

I learned about it by chance and, once again, partly through Léon. A few days after what happened in the café, I happened to meet Charles going into a hotel in the Rue de Turbigo: the Paris-France Hôtel. I was surprised, because when I first came to the workshop, I got the impression that Charles, with the encouragement of M. Albert, had succeeded, after a difficult court case, in getting back the apartment that he had occupied with his wife and children before the war.

Léon then told me that after the regulations were passed on restitution of homes to one of the surviving members of a deported family, several associations were set up. 'Not Jewish associations,' Léon added, 'but Fascist leagues which refused to understand or accept that some Jews did come back. So, to counter the "claims" of Jews who wanted to return to their homes, they set up the League for the Rebirth of the French Home and the Federation of Tenants in Good Faith, which had its headquarters at 10, Rue de Lancry.'

'At 10, Rue de Lancry? Where the Jewish Cultural League used to be?'

'Yes, Monsieur, the very same,' Léon said, putting on a Yiddish accent.

'But why there, of all places?'

'I never found out. But since they organized various demonstrations, always with the same agenda – France for the French, the Jews to the gas ovens and all that – there were raids on the headquarters of the organization and the police found lists of shock troops ready to use force. So finally the organizations were disbanded.'

'What happened to their members?'

'You meet them from time to time in a café, drinking a German beer,' Léon answered, with a smile.

I didn't ask him any more questions. It was he who brought up the subject of Charles again.

'To begin with, when Charles was still saying that he ought perhaps to try to recover his apartment, M. Albert realized that he wouldn't do it. He told me that he thought it would mean that Charles had stopped believing that his family would return. Together, because they both knew that Charles wouldn't go alone, they went to the offices of the UJRE in the Rue de Saintonge and a lawyer took charge of the matter. They had to wait some time, but eventually Charles was able to move back into his apartment. However, in compensation, the landlord was granted a rent of 8,800 francs for the time when Charles was "resident" elsewhere.'

'What about the hotel?'

'The hotel is where Charles came to live at the Liberation and, of course, it's right opposite his apartment. He probably thought that from there he would be better placed to keep watch on comings and goings at the house ... Waiting for someone to come back ... In the end, he just stayed on in the hotel, which costs him 60 francs a day.'

'What about the apartment?'

'It's still there, empty, without curtains in the windows. But there's nothing the landlord can do, because Charles pays the rent regularly. I sometimes walk down Rue de Turbigo, because there's a shop with supplies for the tailoring trade near his house, but I never dare look up at the hotel. I'm too afraid I may see Charles staring out of the window of his room, watching and waiting for someone to appear on the second floor of the building opposite.'

One day, I'm not sure why, Jacqueline asked me, 'When a child dies, what is done with its things?'

I didn't answer. Am I the person to tell her what they do with a child's things, when it dies in its own home?

An Odd One

On the first day, we just told each other our names.

'What's your name?'

'Maurice.'

'I'm Simone.'

And that was more or less all.

She didn't ask questions. That way, I didn't have to make anything up. When I talked, it was fine. Otherwise, nothing. And she didn't tell me any stories about herself. I think that strengthened the bond between us.

For several months I used to go and see her on Sunday mornings. I gave her her money, since it was her job. I put the money on a little table near the bed, knowing that this was how it was done once you knew the price. While I was putting my clothes back on, she stayed there with the sheets and blankets up to her chin. I liked it that way, always leaving with her still in bed.

Simone was not the first I had known.

It was shortly after I came to Paris. I was looking for a place as a machinist at an address I had been given. The job had already gone, but I remembered the name of the street. It's one where there are girls walking up and down. Only after I'd settled into the job at M. Albert's did I go back to the Rue Saint-Denis.

To begin with, I tried a lot of girls. You could almost say that I had a different one each time. Why did I try different ones? I'm not sure that I can really explain. Broadly speaking, I didn't want any complications.

Simone was a redhead. I said to myself: 'Well, why not a redhead?'

The following Sunday, when I walked past her again, she simply took my hand. I didn't try to argue and went upstairs.

That time, she put on a nightdress with thin straps so that I could see her shoulders. She got into bed and then pulled up the sheets. I slipped in next to her.

Usually, afterwards, she just put my head against her breast.

Once, with my head against her breast, I slept for more than an hour. I think she waited for me to wake up of my own accord. Or perhaps she made some movement. Before leaving, I put down a bit more money than usual on the little table. I was afraid she would thank me the following Sunday, but she didn't say anything.

And so for several months she warmed my back with her body.

Then the day came when, putting a hand on my left arm, she said, 'We've got an odd one here all right!' And since I didn't understand, without letting go of my arm, she rolled up my shirt-sleeve.

There was half a minute's silence while I just looked at her, forcing her to explain. She had played the number that they had tattooed on my forearm on the National Lottery, and it lost. Being fond of me, she had thought it would bring her luck, but it hadn't. She was mistaken: they hadn't given me a lucky number.

While she was telling me this, I just listened. I was sitting on her bed, half undressed. I turned my back to her, leaning forwards, as if to put my head in my hands. But I started to fasten the buttons on my shirt-sleeves and then picked up my trousers, which were lying over the back of the chair. I was thinking that I must simply stand up, get dressed and leave the room. Above all, not say anything.

'Are you getting dressed? What's the matter? Why don't you say something?'

I could feel her behind me, sitting up in the bed, while I was putting on my trousers.

'Are you leaving without a word? Don't tell me you're leaving without saying a word! What on earth is going on in that head of yours? If you want people to stop putting their foot in it, perhaps you should have a bit more to say for yourself! After all, you can't spend your whole life feeling miserable. Are you listening to me?'

And because she had a pretty fair idea of what life's about, she offered me a coffee.

I was on the point of saying 'yes', but instead I almost threw myself out of the door. I wanted to wish her good luck and happiness, but I didn't say anything. What goes on in my head, doesn't always want to come out of there, so I'm the one who goes out. I'm not saying it's a good thing; that's just how it is.

It was not until I had shut the door that I realized I had forgotten to give her her money. But I think she would have refused to take it. I remembered it because she had also told me that just because I was paying, it didn't mean I could do whatever I liked: and I was afraid then that she might suddenly tell me all the stories she had kept to herself up to that moment.

On the way down the stairs I wanted to cry, and I wanted to cry when I got out into the street. But, needless to say, I couldn't just lean against a wall, with all those people going past. So I went home.

Lying on my bed, I thought of Simone again. Then I thought of Mme Himmelfarb. It was only when I started to think of her that I finally gave way to grief.

*

It was in 1934, towards the end of the summer, that my mother thought to find me a situation in a tailor's.

I was just fourteen, the age when people used to start as apprentices. Often they went into their father's workshop. But my father was a shoemaker and my mother was determined not to see me sitting, in my turn, on a little low stool, with the muddy shoes of Jews from Szydlowiec in my hands. What's more, she had never been able to stand my father's habit of putting a handful of tacks in his mouth. He found it much more practical to hold them between his lips, the point inwards, and to push them out one by one with his tongue, rather than having to search for them at the bottom of the large cardboard box that he went to buy once a month from a wholesaler from Radom.

'My mouth is a third hand,' he often told my mother.

'The customers can never understand what you're saying, with your mouth full of nails.'

'They understand quite well,' my father answered, clenching his teeth to prevent the tacks from falling out of his mouth.

In any case, both of them were more or less agreed that I should go in for tailoring – my father because his father had been a shoemaker before him, and he thought that we could stop at that; my mother because she was too afraid of having the doctor rushing to the house every time I swallowed a nail, and because she had found a tailor on the far side of town who was willing to take me on as apprentice.

There were plenty of tailors closer to home; but for many of them the first duty of an apprentice was to look after the children of the house, take them to *heder** and sweep the shop. If there was any time left over, and the apprentice was really interested in the trade, he could watch the others working, but without asking too many questions, so as not to distract those whose chief concern was earning a living.

'Let Maurice come with a man's thimble in his size and he will find everything else he needs in the shop.'

So the day after Yom Kippur, sitting on a working stool, with my right foot resting on my left knee and my thimble carefully fitted on my finger, I found myself in Mr Himmelfarb's workshop learning my first stitches.

I had hardly been there an hour when Mrs Himmelfarb came and sat down on a stool opposite me. I should tell you straight away how beautiful she was, but before that – because it will prove to be important – I must mention that her stool was higher than mine, with two sets of bars.

The first look I gave Mrs Himmelfarb was when I heard her say, 'Good morning, Moïshé.' I decided that I ought to return the greeting, so that's what I did.

*Religious infants' school.

After that, I didn't dare look at her, partly because she was so beautiful, and partly because I wanted to concentrate on sewing as Mr Himmelfarb had shown me. He had told me first to practise blind hem stitch, because it's a very important one in made-to-measure tailoring. You have to make the stitches in one layer of fabric and catch only a thread of the fabric underneath it with the needle. I was using white tacking thread, and, as the fabric was black, you could see straight away whether my stitches were too large.

I said that I would tell you how beautiful Mrs Himmelfarb was, but there are no words to convey just how beautiful. Many of her features I have never forgotten, for example her black eyes, which were blacker than any I'd ever seen before. I'd also like . . . I want to describe how her eyes shone, her slightly moist mouth, her skin, which must have been so soft . . . but I can't, because I feel a sort of physical pain, my heart is beating so fast, even today.

It was there, sitting opposite Mrs Himmelfarb, that I did my apprenticeship.

In the mornings she took up her place on the stool a little while after I'd arrived, because before that she was looking after the baby – a little girl. It was only when a young woman came to give her a hand that she would walk down the short corridor separating the apartment from the workshop. Once there, she did whatever work her husband had got ready for her.

This is the point where Mrs Himmelfarb's stool becomes important.

At a bespoke tailor's, when part of a garment has to be sewn by hand, you put it on your knee. Mr Himmelfarb himself would sit on the cutting table in what's known as half tailor position – that is to say, with one leg crossed under him and the other hanging over the edge of the table. However, Mrs Himmelfarb used to steady her knees by resting her heels on the top crossbar of her stool. This meant that, whenever she had to get down from the stool, she would put her feet down one after the other.

On the third day after I joined the Himmelfarbs, as I was starting to have the courage to look up from my work, I thought I noticed, just before she lowered her second leg, that my boss's lovely wife was not wearing any knickers. I say 'I thought I noticed', because that afternoon, when, naturally, I was careful to look up at her each time she got off the stool, I did observe, twice, that Mrs Himmelfarb had on a pair of white knickers. But that in itself was quite something for a fourteen-year-old boy, so much so that immediately – on both occasions – I felt a terrible bulge under my flies, a bulge which seemed to have no intention of going down, to the point where I was obliged to move the fabric up to the top of my thighs, while continuing to practise my hem stitching. I almost shuddered at the mere thought of hearing my boss ask me to fetch something, which would have meant standing up. Imagining the shame that I should have felt if that had happened quelled my extreme arousal.

The next morning, I was able to confirm it: Mrs Himmelfarb really was not wearing any knickers. It was the first time that I had seen the place in question from so close to. My hands began to tremble. I was unable to hold my needle properly or to sew the blind hem stitches as my boss had taught me. I almost ran to the toilets, which, as in almost all the houses in Szydlowiec, were on the half-landings. I undid my flies and the jet spurted against the wall. I had never before sent one so far. I went back upstairs, calm enough to resume my work more or less normally, but, for fear that it might send me rushing down to the toilets once more, I did not dare look up at Mrs Himmelfarb again when she got down from her stool.

That afternoon she had again put on a pair of white knickers. None the less, that didn't stop me slipping out to the toilet in memory of what I had seen that morning.

Even today, when I think of the places where I spent my apprenticeship, I can see that lavatory where on so many occasions I would go and lean against the wall, just as clearly as I can see Mr Himmelfarb's workshop

– because, the next day and the following one, I had the same fleeting vision, with the same unsettling effect.

Several times at first, in reply to my boss's anxious and questioning look, I pretended that I had a tummy upset. But after a while I managed to perform so quickly that the amount of time I spent in the toilets seemed quite normal.

It is now some twelve years since all this and, I can't explain it, but I have such an exact and persistent recollection of the warm image of Mrs Himmelfarb, her feet being placed one after the other on the floor, her black eyes, and her fur, which seemed so soft to me, that this memory is with me still, every time I have the opportunity to discover a woman in her nakedness.

One time – and I am still slightly ashamed to talk about it, because it made me feel so stupid – the lovely Mrs Himmelfarb, after greeting me as always with her 'Good morning, Moïshé' when she came into the room, went straight to her husband, who was working as usual in the room next door, where the cutting table and the sewing machine were. Mechanically, I looked after her and I had only just bent over my work again – 'Italian-style' buttonholes, which I apparently used to do very well – when a muffled little laugh made me look up. Through the open door between the two rooms that made up the workshop, I saw Mr Himmelfarb's hand slip under his wife's skirt. There was no hope of finishing that buttonhole: the trembling that suddenly seized my hands precluded close work of any kind. As on the first day, the excitement that overwhelmed me was almost painful, and once again I realized that only the exercise which I engaged in regularly on the half-landing below would manage to calm me down.

I had the feeling that my penis had never ever been so hard; I had only just started, closing my eyes the better to recall Paradise, when I heard a plop in the water. I leant over, intrigued to know what it was, just in time to see my thimble – which, in my haste, I had forgotten to remove from my finger – disappearing down the pan.

I didn't finish what I had come to do: the feeling had passed. All that was left was to decide how, when I got back upstairs, I would tell them that my thimble had fallen down the lavatory. Especially in front of Mrs Himmelfarb. I didn't dare look at her as I stammered incoherently that my thimble had fallen out of my pocket when I took my trousers down and that I was not in time to catch it. Mr Himmelfarb burst out laughing and opened the drawer in his sewing machine.

'Here,' he said, holding out a thimble, 'take this one. It should be your size. It's the one my father bought me when I was learning the job. Try not to lose it, and then you can pass it on yourself, when you have an apprentice of your own.'

I never did pass the thimble on. I lost it on the train which took us all away when the Germans, with the help of the Polish police, arrested the Jews of Szydlowiec.

Part Two

'You think you are taking your head
in your hands, but it is the head which, like a madman,
chases after the hands.'

PIERRE DUMAYET

'How I long to return to being that child!
He anticipated everything – and that's why he cried.'

JEAN TARDIEU, *First Person Singular*

Extracts from Raphaël's Diary
1981–82

It is now a fortnight since Nathan was buried in the Montparnasse cemetery. A few lines in the obituary column of *Le Monde*, and on that day the Montparnasse cemetery became a meeting place for his friends. It was three o'clock in the afternoon. It was very hot.

Nathan died of the Auschwitz disease.

To celebrate the kind of man he was – and for those who attended his funeral, he was someone important – a few friends came with speeches.

They recalled that he had been an activist who was deeply troubled by the fate of the world, and that he had participated in all the progressive struggles of the post-war period. They spoke of his commitment to the Communist Party.

Others defined him as outraged and indignant. They said, too, that he had an innate sense of justice (which is true) and that he had a profound sense of humour (which is also true, but not so simple). They said that they were surprised, astonished, as though death had struck him suddenly, torn him from life, forgetting that he had already had so much to do with death; forgetting, most of all, that he had been deported at the age of sixteen, and he had never recovered from that.

Their speeches avoided mentioning whatever seemed inexplicable, such as his obstinate refusal to visit Germany, the country he had passed through in 1943 inside a sealed wagon. Anger, discreet but never pacified, prevented him from ever setting foot there. He had experienced the camps, barbed wire, hunger, humiliation. The gas chambers and the crematoria. What he had lived through was unforgettable – but of that, naturally, he said nothing.

At first, when he joined the party, he used to write militant articles in which he measured himself against history. History proved him wrong, because history is the stronger; yet he was right, despite history.

He no longer wrote of anything except what happened every day, only speaking about what is transient and ephemeral. But these ephemeral things were precisely what he could not do without.

This world, he said, can't be changed.

What remained was his loyalty to the comrades he could not forget.

We thought for a long time that he would write the book which would be his testimony and say the things that he did not speak about. Despite our pleas, he never wrote it. He found it more natural to advise us to read Antelme, Primo Levi or Jankélévitch.

One evening, at the Théâtre Récamier, watching one of the rare performances of *And die Musik* by the Pip Simmons group, I noticed that several of our friends were in the audience. That was when I found out that, like me, they had come in response to a persuasive phone call from Nathan.

Many of the same friends were there in the Montparnasse cemetery.

Why did so many of us turn up, when he didn't know that we were there? To say that we loved him? To listen to people saying what they had to say? No doubt it was all done as it had to be done and the words were meant kindly, but what was said could have been said when he was alive.

We shall no longer talk about Nathan except in the past.

I imagined myself with Nathan, back on his feet again, striding along the streets of Ménilmontant. We had been there together, a dozen years earlier, on our way back from the eastern suburbs – I'd been taking some pictures for an article he had to write. We left the car near the metro station at Couronnes so that we could walk as far as the Rue Piat, where he used to live before

the war. It was a long time since he had been back;
now, like others in the district, the street was threatened
with demolition. Oddly enough, a poem by Raymond
Queneau warned him of what was to come. Nathan
frequently read Queneau. I had never met anyone who
knew so many poems by heart as he did. I photographed
him in front of the house where he spent the early
years of his childhood, until his parents were deported;
keeping his cigarette in his mouth, he recited: 'Round
earth, goodbye / Farewell, green trees / I'm off to die /
And greet the worms.' I told him he was a stupid jerk
and took the picture. Some ash fell on his jacket.

The company of a friend gave him a little more strength
to face these streets, to explore them and to search them,
at once fearful and curious, uneasy and affectionate,
recalling the shops, opening the street doors to catch a
glimpse of corridors and gardens, fragments of familiar
spaces, as if in the hope of recapturing for an instant
something – he was not sure what – that was both
intangible and persistent.

Nathan more or less summed up the visit in a word:
we were having coffee in the Repos de la Montagne, a
wine-coloured bistro at the foot of the steps that go up
the Rue Vilin: 'This street's fantastic!'

I have often walked these streets; Nathan was surprised to find that I felt at home here. This is where I took

most of my first photographs. My head full of professional details, I told Nathan that the Repos de la Montagne had been photographed in the 1950s by Willy Ronis and that the house a little further along on the same side, with the closed shutters, had belonged to Mme Rayda, a fortune teller photographed by Robert Doisneau.

At the top of the steps in the Rue Vilin there is a little crossroads from which you get what is possibly the finest view over Paris. There, hard against the railings, is a fine baker's shop, painted ochre, where Nathan went to buy a bar of chocolate. While he was munching it with immense pleasure, I carried on with my list of details, remarking that we were standing on the very spot where Simone Signoret in *Casque d'or* made a horse-drawn cab stop to pick up Serge Reggiani, playing a worker in a joiner's shop run by a larger-than-life Gaston Modot.

'And there,' Nathan replied, 'at the end of the Rue Piat, you can still see the steps that I would go up and down on my way to and from infant school, on the far side of the Rue des Couronnes. I learned to count going up those steps: there are exactly 91 of them.'

I didn't interrupt his memories.

I took some shots of an old café which was shut and in darkness, and of two houses with boarded-up windows. On one of them there was a demolition notice.

I took a few more pictures from the doorway of a third house which had been pulled down, leaving a wasteland already covered with wild grass and rubbish, including an old, rusted wire mattress. Painted on the wall at the back of what must have been a courtyard, the letters 'WC' were still readable, with an arrow below them. There, with a proper regard for decency, a tramp was pissing against the wall. Despite the anecdotal nature of the scene (and I had often told myself that the one thing to be avoided was the picturesque), I couldn't resist it: *click!* Nathan, standing beside me, smiled and said again that the streets were fantastic.

I took some photographs of interior walls partly covered with washed-out, flowered wallpaper, the marks made by the flues and some ceramic tiles with little blue and white lozenges showing very clearly where a kitchen had been.

Today these streets are three-quarters demolished and Nathan never had much inclination to go back. The wrecker's pickaxe will catch up with us, he predicted.

What remains are a few photographs of Nathan as he followed the pavements around the streets of Ménilmontant. From now on his absence is the story they will tell.

Later on, I was looking at all of these photographs while I was meant to be doing some filing – one of those exercises that are never altogether satisfactory, but sometimes produce agreeable surprises; it was then that things fell into place and a mechanism was released that transformed, or rather directed, my work. The effect was so powerful that it resulted in a kind of paralysis – for many weeks I did not take a single photograph; I was searching for a way to photograph not that which existed, but what had disappeared, because I felt the lack of something is what allows us to see it.

It was not until I was in Poland, in the Jewish cemetery at Radom, where all the tombstones have vanished, leaving gaping holes as far as the eye can see, that for the first time I was perhaps able to achieve my aim – to do exactly what I wanted to do as a photographer.

The contents of those holes, revealed in the photographs, is what was once the life of the Jews in Poland.

It was during this period of paralysis that I started to make notes, in order to avoid being completely discouraged. It was not that I was trying to keep a 'diary'. And I was certainly not trying to substitute writing for photography, even temporarily. So: no ink (which is a sort of step towards printed matter), but black Conté HB pencils, evenly sharpened.

Until then, for my photography I had only ever

written – in ink, this time – notes for my files, giving subject, place, date, time if I considered it important, and lens (though rarely, because I don't like wide angles or long focus, so I often use the same lens).

Now I write, but I don't write about what happens, and, in particular, I don't write about what happens to me.

The notes I make, when it comes down to it, contain only a few things from my life and – this is the only way I can put it – run alongside the photographs that I might take. The words that I string together, events or memories, like the steps that I take when I am walking idly around Paris, invariably help me to rediscover the road back to photography.

And I don't attempt to assess whether I am making progress in the practice of writing, even if, occasionally, caught up in the game – or caught in the trap? – of writing, I look in the dictionary, cross out, rewrite, sharpen my pencil, put a full stop and start a new paragraph.

Of the friends who came to Nathan's funeral, it was a young man who closed the parenthesis of this common past. He went over to the coffin, like someone crossing to the far bank of a river. He had a cello in his hand. And he spoke:

'I did not know Nathan well. I just used to see him

from time to time when he came to dinner with my parents. So I have a few fragmentary memories of him. But the impression that he made was so strong that I made sure I was there every time he came, just to be there, to listen to him. Yet he spoke very little . . . One evening, he had arrived a bit early, when I was half-heartedly trying to learn a Yiddish lullaby. Nathan came over to listen, and signalled to me to carry on. But I was shy, so I stopped playing; he just said that one day, when I knew it well, he would be happy to listen to the piece, which he was very fond of. Rather stupidly, I thought he was saying this out of kindness, to encourage me, so I didn't learn the lullaby straight away, as I should have done. When I learned that Nathan was ill, I went back to studying it seriously. But by then it was too late. Nathan was too sick to come to our house again, for me to play the lullaby to him as he had requested. So all I can do today is to sit beside him and play this Yiddish lullaby for him. I think he would have liked that. The chorus ends, each time, with, "Sleep, little Jew, sleep." It is called *Rozhinkès mit Mandlen* . . . I also want to say that I should have liked to speak these few words in Yiddish, because that was the language of the time when he, too, was living with his parents . . . the language of the time when he was fully alive. But that's something I cannot do.'

Nathan had his speech in Yiddish: from the lips of

those who remembered came a few words of the lullaby: '*Unter uideles Vigele . . . Shteyt a klor-vays tsigele . . . Dos vet zayn dayn baruf . . . Rozhinkès mit mandlen . . . Shlof zhe, Yidele, shlof . . .*'

Those who did not understand listened to the words and at the end everyone gave way to grief. After that, we threw the roses into the grave.

There was no photograph of Nathan dead. Nor are there any pictures which will one day say: 'Look at these faces. Nathan is dead and it is the grief caused by his death that these photographs describe.'

I have found the poem by Queneau which alerted Nathan to what was to come. It is 'Slum Clearance' in *Courir les rues*, published by Gallimard in 1967.

Appeal for offers
demolition work
insalubrious precinct No 7
(only in time of war do we hear vociferation
when salubrious precincts come up for demolition)
the tract in question lies within the cincture of the Rue des
    Couronnes the Rue Julien-Lacroix
the Rue d'Eupatoria the Rue de la Mare and the Passage
    Notre-Dame-de-Lacroix
must go and see before it all disappears.

So Nathan had gone to 'see before it all disappears'.

Can one photograph everything? Not everything, surely? Could I have photographed Nathan's funeral? And taken photos that were right? Suppose another photographer had happened to go past, not knowing anyone: what would he have photographed? What would he have shown of our grief? But then, perhaps, because he didn't know anyone, he might have been able to do it. For how can one be on both sides at once? How can one be part of the event, living it, and at the same time watch it and fix it on film?

The great photographs, strong photographs that tell us about death, are war photos, those which show violent death.

These victims lying on the ground, their faces turned towards the stars: if you know their names and those of their children, if you know the woman who discovers her husband's body during a civil war, or the starving child next to its dead mother, then surely you cease at that very moment to be a photographer? So, in order to continue being one, you don't stop, you follow the cries, you leave your emotions behind and carry on taking strong photos, which will perhaps bear witness to the misfortunes of the world.

As for a body, and the representation of an ordinary death, I can only think of the portrait that Claude Monet made of his wife Camille on her death bed. Much later, he confessed in a letter to Clemenceau:

. . . so much so that one day, finding myself at the side of a dead woman who had been, and still was, very dear to me, I caught myself in the act of staring at the temple of the tragic head, hunting for the succession and appropriate gradations of hue that death had just imposed on this motionless face.

In front of his dead wife, Monet could not restrain himself from picking up his brushes – not in order to remember her better, but because analysing colours was something that preoccupied every moment of his life. It was stronger than his grief. It is because Claude Monet never ceased to be a painter that he made his wife's death into a work of art to be hung on the wall of a museum.

I am looking once again through the great volume of photographs by Robert Capa; and, once more, I stop at a photograph of which I am particularly fond. This time, however, I want to know why I like this particular picture so much. What is it of? It shows us three small girls. Two of them are holding the hands of an American GI. The third is looking intently at him.

Everything that the photograph has to say, everything that draws one's attention to it, is contained in the looks on those four faces.

The caption reads: 'London, January/February 1943. An American soldier with war orphans "adopted" by his unit.'

I look at the photo again in the light of the caption. The girls are wearing the same lace-up shoes, their coats are similar and they have the same little dresses buttoned high at the front. Their clothes, just like the soldier's uniform, make them recognizable.

You could talk about this photograph in terms of its composition – a triangle with the soldier's face at the top and the bottom being not the feet, but the line of the hands.

What is happening in the photograph follows the sides of the triangle very precisely: the girl who is not holding anyone's hand is standing on the far right of the soldier; the girl on the soldier's left is gripping his hand very tightly because he is looking away from her, and her little clenched hand contradicts her smile; and, finally, the girl who is reassured by the look that the soldier is giving her, and by his hand around hers, is able to smile at the photographer. These three small girls, beneath their trusting smiles, are telling us about the loss of their parents.

If I had read the picture in this way a dozen years ago, at a time when taking photographs no longer seemed to make much sense to me, it would have helped me considerably in the exercise of my profession.

I promise myself that I will start again.

I remember – it must have been when I was twelve – getting up one night to fill a glass of water from the kitchen tap. On the sideboard in the dining room, in a metal dish, a candle was burning. I assumed it had been forgotten and, thinking I was doing the right thing, I put it out. Yet I knew that it had been lit to mark the anniversary of the death of my mother's father and her young brother (a notional anniversary, since they had been deported). In the morning my mother simply told me that I should not have put it out. I would have preferred to be punished. I can still see her astonished look and her sadness. I can still see all her gestures, with extraordinary precision: she goes to fetch the big box of matches that is always kept next to the cooker. She stands, almost leaning against the sideboard, with her back to me. She bends over the candle. She enfolds it with a sort of protective warmth. The wall is lit up by the flickering flame. My mother stays beside it for a long time. She is wearing a handknitted cardigan in beige wool, below which hang two narrow strips of flower-patterned cloth, the ties of her apron. I think she is crying.

That was the day when I really mourned the deaths of my maternal grandfather and uncle, though I had never known them.

*

Anti-Semitic slogans have just been found on the walls of the offices of the UJRE at 14, Rue de Paradis. I learn about it through a phone call from Anna, who was informed by the caretaker at the building. She has asked if I am free to take some photographs. Ten minutes later, after picking up my mail, I am on my way up the Boulevard Magenta on my moped. There is a card from Australia. It is from Georges, with the following few words on the back:

I've been to Sydney, Melbourne, Adelaide, Perth and Brisbane.
    Georges

The vaulted passageway leading into number 14 ends in a little courtyard, on the left of which there is a covered area with some lavatories. It is here, at the bottom of the steps leading into block C, that the vandals have given free rein to their feelings: 'Death to the Jews! Yids out! Jews to the gas chambers!' And, of course, the inevitable 'France for the French'.

The police have also been informed and have already arrived to start their enquiries. The caretaker didn't hear anything.

Other people have gathered, too. A few friends, close neighbours who have come, as people say, to express their indignation. And others who work there, like the old activist, a former deportee, whom I recognize, who is now a receptionist at the dispensary on the second floor.

'You must wipe it all off!' he shouts, while I am trying to take some pictures. 'Wipe it all off!'

'Oh, no,' someone else says. 'It should all be left on. Let people have a look at what these Fascists are capable of!'

'Do you think the people who come here don't know that already? And do you think I'm going to put up with having to read "Death to the Jews!" every time I come down for a piss?'

'It will be washed off,' Anna says, interrupting. 'But first Raphaël is going to take some pictures.'

'Hurrah!'

I have forgotten the old activist's name, but when I hear him shout I remember seeing him just after the war at a film screening held to benefit the children in CCE homes. He suddenly got up, shouting, 'Stop the film! Stop the film! I recognized my father! Stop the film!' On the screen you could see a column of deportees, many of whom were collapsing from exhaustion. They didn't stop the film.

I take another look at Georges's card, which I glanced at rather hurriedly this morning. On the front, to the left, is a photo of two koalas: a baby koala on its mother's back. On the right, some facts about the koala. For practice. I try to translate:

How did the koala get its name? The Australian aborigines used the word "koala" when they didn't want to drink out of a communal vessel. They became accustomed to use the same word to designate the climbing animal that never drinks: the koala.

Known to the first colonists as a local Australian bear, the koala is not in fact a bear, but a marsupial. It weighs between 5½ and 13 kilos and eats nearly a kilo of leaves a day. At birth, the baby koala is the size of a two-cent piece, weighs 5½ grammes and measures 2 centimetres in length. After spending six months in its mother's pouch, the baby climbs up on to her back.

At the age of one year, it has to leave its mother to manage on its own and find its own tree.

More graffiti. This time in Bagneux, at the Paris cemetery of Bagneux.

I know the way there very well. From the Porte d'Orléans, you just have to go through Montrouge. I'm used to it. I go there once a year.

Every year, at the Bagneux cemetery, between Rosh Hashana and Yom Kippur, the Jewish community gathers to remember its dead. For every town, for every village, there is a monument, and, on each monument, names. Carved names. The list of those who have no graves. And they simply read out the names, all the names carved there, without missing a single one.

But before that there is an official ceremony in front of the monument to the Jewish Veterans, which involves speeches and the Kaddish.

Earlier still, we meet in the Balto, the café on the Avenue Marx-Dormoy just opposite the main entrance to the cemetery. The four billiard tables at the back of the room are each covered with a board, like four serving tables. Despite that, there will soon be no seats left, and we shall drink tea while eating pickelfleish sandwiches, which the smart owner of a delicatessen has come to sell at the café door.

'How's the pickel this year?'

'Like every other year.'

On the pavement in front of the Balto, Warga's, the undertaker's is handing out its calendars. Opposite, lined up in a row against the outer wall of the cemetery, are a few dozen banners inscribed in gold letters, one for each mutual aid society: the Brest-Litovsk Friendly Society, the Children of Kielce, the Natives of Lublin, the Friends of Demblin, the Friends of Lask, the Friends of Lubartow, of Plock, of Szydlowiec, of Bendzin, of Radom . . .

'So Raphaël, we haven't seen your parents yet today?'

It's Etner, the president of the Radom Mutual Aid Society.

'They're in Tel Aviv, for the bar mitzvah of Samuel, Betty's son.'

'He's sixteen already? *Mazel tov!* And when will you be coming to our meetings? You know we need young people like yourself . . . with all that's going on . . . Did you see the state of the tombs? You haven't got your camera?'

No, I haven't got my camera.

There is a label pinned to his chest: 'Remember! 6,000,000 victims of Nazi barbarism.' Here, it would be hard to forget. Especially with what's going on. Like the walls of the UJRE offices, seventy tombs in the cemetery have been desecrated: seventy tombs covered with anti-Semitic graffiti.

Every year the Jewish community was chiefly happy to meet here. This year, its members are hurrying indignantly towards Sector 115. They want to see, as if to confirm what they already know. The newspapers have been talking about splinter groups of extremists, but here people have long known what such groups become and what they can do. The tombs in Bagneux bear the names of victims of what once, in Germany at the start of the 1920s, was still only a tiny faction.

The path through Sector 115 is not wide enough to contain the crowd moving around among the tombs. A woman is trying to wipe off a swastika covering several names with her handkerchief. She fails. She scratches it with her nail and still doesn't succeed.

Mechanically, I put my hand to the place on my chest where my Leica usually hangs.

This year in Bagneux the crowd massing around the monument to the Jewish veterans is larger and listens more carefully to the speeches. As usual, the President of the Union of Jewish Societies in France – though more emotional than normal – introduces a succession of figures representing the community. Of course, their speeches warn us to be on our guard, but they are rather disappointing: too official and basically no different from the speeches made in previous years.

Then comes the speech in Yiddish which reawakens our feelings. It is the passion it arouses that makes me listen, even though I do not understand everything. Naturally, there are still speeches in Yiddish from time to time, but only from time to time. So I'm not just listening to the words; I'm listening to the language.

The speaker is an old man, but he has lost none of the force of his indignation. For year after year, he was in every conflict, in every struggle. I know him well: in 1945 he was the one who came to speak at the fête of the summer camp; and even then we called him by his first name: Moïshé.

A worker, a Jew, and for many years an exemplary Communist, he has lived a life which seems to reflect the special relationship of the Jews with history: pogroms in Poland and clandestine meetings, strikes and imprison-

ment, demonstrations and, again, prison. And emi-
gration. A clothing worker in Poland, a clothing worker
in France, a Communist activist in Warsaw, a Communist activist in Paris on the committee of the MOI
(*Main d'Oeuvre Immigrée*: Immigrant Labour), expelled to
become an activist in the Red Cross in Brussels. Then
Spain, with the International Brigades, and then the
Resistance in France. After that, the Liberation and
renewed hope, return to Poland and disappointment.
Back to France in 1968 and today, his heart in Israel,
on the side of the 'Doves' – because Moïshé is not the
sort to say: 'I won't fall for that again!' Because of his
generosity, he has fallen each time for great causes. And
it was this tremendous generosity that meant he could
still, at nearly eighty years of age, find a cause to defend:
and always with the same militant passion and tenacity.

As much as tradition, language and culture, it is
his successive struggles and disillusionments that have
forged his identity. And seeing this old militant, the
pages of his speech fluttering in his trembling hands, I
also understand that, as with Nathan, all his failures are
primarily the failures of our century, and that, too, is
what is handed down to us.

At the very moment when old Moïshé starts to talk
about the scandal of the desecrated tombs, the tip of
one of the burning torches which four Jewish veterans
have been holding since the start of the ceremony falls

to the ground. And, because of the resin or the wax with which these torches are impregnated, the grass catches fire rather alarmingly. Well, one cannot simply leave this piece of torch to burn away in the grass, so the man who has the rest of it still burning in his hand decides to put the fire out by stamping on it. And there, right beside Moïshé, who is just raising his voice, the man (dressed for the occasion in the freshly ironed jacket of a former deportee) is stamping with both feet on the ground because he knows that he really must put out this fire, which is disturbing Moïshé at the very moment when he is conjuring up the spectre of the rebirth of Fascism.

The crowd is silent, its attention divided, one must admit, by the unexpected and unusual spectacle in front of it. What in other circumstances might have been greeted by mild amusement, has the effect here of evoking slightly uneasy curiosity. The assembled community looks at Moïshé who, in his turn, is casting a furious look at the former deportee – still hard at work, almost dancing on the flames which refuse to go out and continue to fuel Moïshé's anger. And the people are unable to concentrate on the speech, which at that very moment is underlining the dangers that threaten us and also calling for vigilance. They are absolutely fascinated by the spectacle of two men, standing side by side, two old Jews whose lives are complete, who are both trying to finish what they have started: one, his speech: the other, putting out the fire.

And it was only when Moïshé wished us a happy new year that the last sparks died, leaving a large brown patch on the ground.

After that, there was the El Mole Ra'hamim, the prayer for the dead: 'El Mole Ra'hamim scho'hen ba-me-romim . . .' I only know the beginning (I don't understand Hebrew), but I know very precisely when and in which order we get to the words Auschwitz, Maidanek, Treblinka, Chelmno, Babi Yar, Warsaw Ghetto . . .

As soon as the prayer for the dead is finished, the members of each Mutual Aid Society gather behind their respective banners; now it is time for the second part of the ceremony, the part which concerns our own families, which is the main reason we have come here.

Like one of those tourist trails where nothing ever changes, the route is always the same: the Avenue of the Dutch Limes, the Avenue of the Flowering Cherries, the Avenue of the Purple Maples, the Avenue of the Black Walnut Trees. These are the names of the paths along the usual route taken by the societies that make up Sector 31. If they were to raise their heads a little, those who follow this itinerary would see, between the trunks of the walnut trees, which are still covered with leaves at Yom Kippur, the serried ranks of artificial flowers and crosses marking the graves of the Catholic sectors.

We talk about work and children, illness and occupied territories. And desecrated tombs. The events of a whole year in a single conversation.

> *Akierman Berek*
> *Akierman Kopek, Fanny and their son*
> *Berneman Rachel*
> *Berneman Nathan, Thérèse and Ida*
> *Berneman Itzek, Chaja and six children*
> *Berneman Moszek and his family*
> *Berneman Nachman and his family*

There are a few dozen of us in the Society of Friends of Radom clustered around the monument to those from the town. From a little square-ruled notebook, the secretary of the society reads the names in the order in which they are inscribed on the black marble of the vault, in a loud voice, so that they can be clearly heard.

> *Etner Fishel, Berger, Lejzer*
> *Epsztein Icek, Drezla, Herchel*
> *Epsztein Pinkus, Etl and Fajga*
> *Frydman Joseph and his family*
> *Frydman Hersch, Perla and Bronka . . .*

Then there was a short silence. After that, without moving from the spot, the secretary handed the little notebook to Etner, who was right beside him – and clearly expecting this – pointing out with his finger the exact place he had reached in the list of names. This was so that he could hear the name of his own family, five times: his father, his mother, his brother, and also his wife and son.

'It's the same every year. When he reaches his own name, only tears come.'

The comment was made by a woman near me.

Etner continued with the reading.

All around us, like an echo, from one monument to the next we could hear the same litany of names: a murmuring sound on which everyone seemed to hang, a sound which told the same story, known to all of us here for so long, and uniting all those present.

After I had heard the name of my grandparents I looked towards the Society of Friends of Siedlec. M. Charles was there, listening. I went over.

'Monsieur Charles?'

'It's you. Hello, Raphaël.'

'How are you?'

'Well, very well.'

I couldn't think of anyone to enquire after, so I didn't ask him for any news. The names of those from the town of Siedlec filled the silence.

Like my father, M. Charles was wearing a 'bespoke' suit, of the kind that people still used to have made for themselves twenty years ago, on the occasion of a Society of Friends dance. M. Charles's suit was far from new. Under the jacket he had put on a thick pullover with a V neck, which showed his tie.

With the Siedlec Society, the names were not read in alphabetical order, but at the letter G, M. Charles half-closed his eyes. His name was spoken three times.

'My wife and my two daughters,' M. Charles said.

'Yes . . . I heard . . .'

I told myself that one had to trust in what was going on around.

'How did the bar mitzvah go?' Charles asked, but only after a pause.

With M. Charles, I was happier when he was the one asking the questions – when the first words came from him. So very quickly, and in a low voice because of the reading, I told him everything that my mother had told me over the phone: about the party, the presents and how happy everyone was.

'Yes, I got a postcard,' Charles said. 'They seemed pleased.'

From the direction of Siedlec, I could hear Kirzenbaum, and from Radom, Lublinski. There are the words that are spoken and there are all the things one hears in one's head.

Sometimes in cemeteries people talk to the bodies of the dead: sitting on a little folding stool, they keep them in touch with what is going on. Who's still alive and who's dead. Who is married and who has a child. Because you want to fill the void, you try to carry on the interrupted dialogue, to feel a presence.

At the cemetery in Bagneux, one always stands. There are tombstones, but no one underneath. No one is buried there. This is all you can say. They are not there, they have never been there. The monuments of the societies whose survivors gather every year are tombs for absent bodies. The bodies of the dead are inaccessible; this is what is unacceptable, and this is why they read out aloud the names inscribed on the stone.

When they had all been read, we left quietly; and, because we are also creatures of memory, we stop at the Balto to exchange a few reminiscences.

But perhaps those who stop off there have come primarily to discover how we are all doing. For no other reason. When it comes to remembering, to ask how someone is, is still the best one can do.

Charles didn't come to the Balto. He was sitting on a bench, apparently waiting for a bus. That's where I saw him when I left. With my car stuck in a traffic jam on the Avenue Marx-Dormoy.

The sky had turned grey. Driven by a light wind, the clouds seemed to pause for a moment above Bagneux. It was raining slightly, a fine, soft rain that Charles seemed not to notice. Perhaps he could not feel it because of his hat.

He did not respond to my wave. Perhaps the only thing to do was to leave him with his sadness, since he could not rid himself of it: a sadness that filled his eyes and extended into some horizon beyond what he could see.

Behind me, a few cars gave vent to their impatience by sounding their horns. I started my windscreen wipers and left Charles sitting on the bench; beside him, utterly useless, stood his folded umbrella.

A new year was starting.

I went to see M. Charles this afternoon. He is in a retirement home for old Jews.

'He must be seventy-eight or seventy-nine,' my mother said. 'He didn't have to go there,' she added. 'He's not ill and he has lots of friends; but he's so stubborn.' And she gave me a cake for him.

To be quite frank, it wasn't only to see M. Charles that I went to the old people's home. I've long had plans, as part of an ongoing project, to photograph old Jews who speak with foreign accents: to photograph these old Jews who still carry within themselves the world which they left behind – a world from which some of them had broken away, which has now been destroyed. There you have it: to take photos and (sorry about the cliché, but I can't think of an alternative) to find my place in their history.

What struck me immediately on entering M. Charles's room was the absence of any personal belongings. There was not even a photo in a frame on the bedside table. There was just a bedside table, a low table, a single bed, a small wardrobe, two chairs and a light armchair, in which Charles was sitting.

On the low table was a little fruit bowl with three apples: Golden Delicious. And an ashtray, because in order to have a room to himself, M. Charles decided to take up smoking.

But there was one surprising object, which must have been unique. On a wooden shelf supported by metal brackets was a sort of Aunt Sally, such as one can still see from time to time in fairgrounds. What was peculiar about this one was that it represented crudely drawn, but perfectly recognizable, war criminals: Hitler, Mussolini, Pétain, Goering, Goebbels, Laval, Doriot . . .

'Do you recognize them?'

'Not all. I don't know who that is, next to Goebbels.'

'Himmler.'

'And next to Doriot?'

'Déat and Darnand. And there are plenty who are not there, who died in their beds, or who were eating croissants for breakfast this morning.'

Charles began to take cloth balls out of a basket beside him. He threw them without taking aim. Sometimes he would throw two at once. Some hit the target and the heads, attached by hinges, fell backwards.

'How did you come by this?'

'I bought it.'

'Where?'

'Where? Who from? How much? What does it matter? I bought it, that's all.'

'And the balls?'

'They came with it.'

Charles had exhausted his supply of balls and the heads were almost all down. I put them back up and returned the balls, which were scattered around the room, to their basket. I was still on all fours recovering the ones that had rolled under the bed when a woman in a nurse's uniform brought in a tray.

'Here you are, Monsieur Charles: tea for two people, as you requested.' And, turning to me: 'Well, now, if you start that, you'll never finish. Monsieur Charles is like a child: every time you pick them up, he throws them again. And, what's more, he cheats: he throws several at a time.'

'Cheat? Me? Do I cheat? Who's cheating here? Huh? Who's cheating here? Who's cheating here?' And with each 'Who's cheating here?' a ball smashed into the Aunt Sally.

The nurse went out, shaking her head, and Charles eventually wiped his face, which was covered in sweat.

'Good, now we can drink our tea,' he said, also wiping his glasses. He went to look for a knife in the drawer of the bedside table, produced half a lemon hidden behind one of the apples in the fruit bowl – 'Would you like some lemon?' – and conscientiously cut two slices off it. Then he cut up the cake.

'Have a piece.'

'No, no. It's for you.'

'Eat it! It's too much for me.'

'You can share it with the others.'

'So that they can say they used to have better at home? Eat it!'

We ate in silence.

After a short while I told Charles that I would come back a few times – to see him and because I had the photos to take. I stayed a little longer, then I did as I had said and got up to leave.

Charles took a ball for the Aunt Sally and he, too, stood up.

'Choose a head.'

'Pétain.'

His aim was perfect and the ball struck Pétain's forehead with a dull sound. The old bastard went *clack!*

At that moment I knew (but did I still doubt it?) that I should very soon return.

The old Jews in the retirement home who were not in their rooms were in the main hall, sitting on seats lined up around the walls.

Like children in the playground of an infant school waiting at half-past four for someone to collect them, they were sitting one beside the other. There was even one little old lady whose feet hardly touched the ground, who seemed ready to leave. Even though it was summer, she was wearing a coat and had a handbag on her knees. From time to time, at regular intervals, her lips would move. I assumed she was conversing with the past, with those memories that are fixed once and for all. She made a whole series of little movements: opening her handbag, putting her right hand into it, without ceasing to mutter, taking out a bunch of keys, looking at them for a while, then putting them back at the bottom of the bag, which she snapped shut. And then it would all begin again, the same gestures, repeated in exactly the same way. Time, her time, seemed to move to the rhythm of these few movements.

As I went past her to get to the front door, I felt myself starting to shake: what the little old Jewess kept on repeating at perfectly regular intervals – which I had imagined to be the story of a long career – I could now hear quite clearly and precisely: it was just one word, always the same and always said twice in succession, the word with which she had so often greeted us: 'Hello-hello'.

Yesterday evening I was watching a broadcast on the third programme, F R 3, about the children of deportees. It was being repeated to mark the fortieth anniversary of the round-up at the Vel' d'Hiv. The first time it was shown was in 1971. I'm watching it again on the video: here is the end:

We have heard from Bernadette, Liliane, Simone, Janine and Nadia, and perhaps through them we have heard the others: those men and women whom I did not go to see or who refused to come; those who, as they say, found it harder to get through it, and who are in the majority. And then, perhaps, we may have heard, faintly, the voice of Marcel, to whom this programme is dedicated.

He arrived at Andresy in 1945, together with the rest. He was six. While his comrades were already settling in, he kept apart, standing with his back to a tree and crying. He was inconsolable. He didn't want to go inside this house, which was too large for him, this house that in no way reminded him of the one where he had spent his early childhood.

There are some people who are immediately attractive. Marcel was one of them. But all the affection that surrounded him could not prevent him from being alone. One day, in November 1963,

*he killed himself in the park outside the manor of Andresy. He
was twenty-four.*

*I don't know if any death can be explained and no doubt it
is better not to try. However, since I learned of this death I have
not been able to forget it. Perhaps this is because Marcel did not
die on 26 November 1963, but had already been killed with his
parents, a little over twenty-five years ago.*

This morning, received a letter from the club for former
residents of CCE homes, about the annual meeting,
with the date and venue where it will take place. Then
the following:

*Price of entry: a family photo, especially one showing your children
and grandchildren. We want to build up a great album, in the
form of a mural, which will fill up progressively as you arrive.*

On behalf of the Amicale des Anciens:

*Annette P. – Emile J. – Paulette C. – René K. – Rosette
T. – Rosette B. – Georges P. – Simon G. – Simone M.*